Scan the QR Code below
for more information
on Terry's work:

Quotation Sources by Permission:

BSB Berean Study Bible © 2016, 2020. Bible Hub.

CSB Christian Standard Bible © 2017. Holman Bible Publishers.

ESV The Holy Bible, English Standard Version © 2001. Crossway, a publishing ministry of Good News Publishers.

KJV King James Version.

NIV The Holy Bible, New International Version © 1973, 1978, 1984. International Bible Society.

NLT The New Living Translation © 1996, 2004, 2007, 2013, 2015. Tyndale House Foundation. Tyndale House Publishers.

All other quotes from songs, lyrics, poetry, and prose are in public domain.

Cover and interior design by Kathryn Krogh
Author photo by Kimberly Krauk

ISBN: 978-1-7341122-5-2

To:

_____

From:

_____

Date:

_____

Moon River

God Hears You!
Do You Hear God?

Terry Ward Tucker

TERRY WARD
TUCKER

— *Anne* —

My name is Anne York, and this is my story. I am sharing it with you, because I want you to know you are not alone in heartache. How can I be sure? Well, I'm your friend now, which means you have a warm connection you did not have before.

I am the woman you thought had everything, whose life seemed perfect while yours was forevermore imploding. But I assure you, I have never had everything. Indeed, my life has been far from perfect, my decisions seldom wise, and my heart often drowning in turmoil. Truth? I've made a mess of most things I have tried to accomplish, all without God, of course, so many that I've been hesitant to fling back the curtain and expose my failures to the light of day. Not until I remembered you, and that same old familiar pain on your face you have always tried to hide, did I realize I had no choice but to speak out. I had to make certain you knew you were not the only one prone to stumbling into dark pits. The Good News is you no longer must endure hard times alone, for I know and can affirm that God in Jesus, by the power and presence of the Holy Spirit, is your loving friend and Savior, as he is mine. He will comfort you and light your way, as he does for me. And he will help you if you ask him, no matter how faint your call, just as he helps me.

So then, the time has come for you to consider some important questions. When God speaks to you, can you hear him, commune with him, submit to him, know, love, and obey him? And if you cannot, are you willing to respond to his love-inspired, light-inspired, life-inspired, grace-inspired,

Father-inspired, Jesus-inspired, Spirit-inspired promptings to learn how? I pray with all my heart you will answer yes. Your life depends on it now and forever. God hears you! Do you hear God?

Then you will call upon me and come and pray to me,
and I will hear you.
JEREMIAH 29:12 ESV

But as for me, I watch in hope for the Lord. I wait
for God my Savior; my God will hear me.
MICAH 7:7 NIV

I love the Lord because he hears my voice and my prayer
for mercy. Because he bends down to listen,
I will pray as long as I have breath!
PSALM 116:1-2 NLT

As he (Jesus) was speaking, a woman in the crowd called
out, "God bless your mother - the womb from which you
came, and the breasts that nursed you!" Jesus replied,
"But even more blessed are all who hear the word
of God and put it into practice."
LUKE 11:27-28 NLT

Chapter

1

Tidying up the space around the altar of his beloved church, *New Light Tabernacle,* had never been a burden to Pastor Mason Seabrook, and this night was no exception. He needed the quiet routine to help him wind down after being tormented two hours by the budget committee, members of which did not bring to mind the attribute of saintliness. Over his three-and-a-half decades at *New Light,* Pastor Seabrook had seen budget committees, and every other kind of committee, come and go. Yet, somehow, he had managed to transcend the endless initiatives, action plans, programs, campaigns, and modern innovations and keep his mind and heart on Jesus.

The good pastor always saved straightening the altar table for last before leaving the sanctuary. Flower arrangements so bright and fresh on Sunday mornings were no longer lively by midweek. Years ago, the quiet pastor had taken it as his personal duty, whenever the flowers began to shed, to gather up the stray petals and deposit them back into the altar vase for lack of a trash receptacle in the worship area. All other housekeeping tasks he left to Berta, *New Light*'s aging German cleaning lady, who came nightly to mop the sanctuary floor and daily to do everything else.

After putting the altar table back to rights and mumbling a quick prayer, the silver-haired clergyman shuffled over to the side exit near the pipe organ, where he stopped to glance over his shoulder at his handiwork. Satisfied all was well, unaware he had forgotten for the first time in thirty-five years to lock the front entrance to the vestibule, he clicked the side door shut behind him and trudged down the long hallway toward his study, where good books and hot tea awaited the weariest preacher in Savannah.

❦

An hour after Pastor Seabrook left the sanctuary, Berta, *New Light*'s only sanitation employee, entered the door of her boss' departure. She brought with her the same old rolling metal bucket she had used for years to do her mopping. As always, she backed through the doorway to keep from sloshing soapy water onto the hardwood. Berta's decade-long procedure progressed in the same manner as every other evening, until she noticed an odd glimmer in the brass base of a tall candle holder next to the exit.

On turning to look, she took a quick step back, startled to discover the source of the strange reflection. On the floor just beyond the top altar step glowed a semicircle of lit candles. But more disturbing than the fire hazard was a human form lying face down across the three steps leading to the altar.

With a muffled yelp and a clatter of equipment, Berta deserted her mop and bucket and rushed back through the doorway she had just entered.

❦

Pastor Seabrook, who had not gotten through the first ten

pages of *Mere Christianity* by C.S. Lewis before falling asleep in his leather desk chair, jolted awake to the sound of someone pounding on his study door. It was Berta, agitated and insistent, yet unable to communicate her problem to the pastor in neither her native German nor broken English. Pastor Seabrook had no alternative but to follow her back to the sanctuary, his heart pounding at what he might encounter in that hallowed space.

He could never have imagined the scene he came upon, beautiful and terrible at the same time. Candlelight, enchanting and dangerous, shone dreamlike on the motionless body of the loveliest of intruders, making her crime of breaking and entering seem almost a blessing.

Pastor Seabrook signaled Berta to wait by the door while he approached the young woman on the steps. Kneeling beside her, he brushed back her hair. She stirred and tried to sit up, resisting the pastor's kind hand. It was then he recognized her face. "Anne...Anne York?" he said. "What are you doing here, Annie?"

The young woman moaned and tried to pull away, but the pastor would not let go of her shoulders until she relaxed. "This isn't like you," he said. "Are you sick...on meds? What's the matter?"

Anne responded in a slur. "Yes...sick...dying."

Pastor Seabrook loosened his grip and allowed her to sit on her own, though he did not stop trying to help. "Do you want me to call Gabe...or someone else in your family?"

"No, no. I'm all right," she said. "I just need to go home, get some rest." She stood, though unsteady, and retrieved her tote bag from the bottom step.

Pastor Seabrook stood with her. "I'll check on you in the morning," he said, "if you promise to go straight home. It's late...dark out."

"I will...promise. Thank you, pastor. Thanks."

"Maybe I should drive you. I'm not comfortable, your leaving alone, not when you're ill like this."

Anne shook herself to sharpen her wits. "No, my car is right out front. Lots of streetlights. I'm fine now, really."

Pastor Seabrook looked uncertain, but he did not argue. "I'll call then," he said, "if you're sure you'll be okay driving."

Anne hugged her dear shepherd, after which she slumped over like a much older woman and made her way toward the vestibule doors. Once there, she glanced back at Pastor Seabrook and waved goodbye with a weak hand and a weaker smile. He nodded and returned her wave, though not her smile. Anne hesitated a brief moment before disappearing into the night.

⟨⟨⟨⟨

Pastor Seabrook's usual serene face now looked worried. It was clear from the set of his shoulders he was overtired. And straightening the sanctuary a second time added more strain, what with the candles and smokiness and dripping wax.

Berta, who from the side exit had observed the peculiar exchange between the pastor and Anne, shuffled over to help her old friend. When all was orderly again, Pastor Seabrook thanked Berta and excused her from mopping, a first. Berta hustled out the side exit before he changed his mind, leaving him alone to lock up and turn out the lights. On his way back from securing the vestibule doors, he spied an envelope in the shadow of the second altar step. He picked it up and studied the block lettering on the front: ANNE'S VOW BEFORE GOD. Curiosity getting the better of him, he slipped the document from the envelope and unfolded it. He read a few words aloud before sitting down on the top step to read the rest.

1 SAMUEL 1:10-11a "In her deep anguish, Hannah prayed to the Lord, weeping bitterly. And she made a vow, saying, 'Lord Almighty, if you will only look upon your servant's misery and remember me, and not forget your servant but give her a son, then I will give him to the Lord for all the days of his life.'"

At the bottom of the page, just below the Scripture passage, Anne had added a prayer of her own, which Pastor Seabrook also read aloud. *"Dear God, it's Anne praying now, not Hannah. I'm begging you to hear me. Hannah asked you for a son so long ago in the Old Testament. And you granted mercy and sent her a baby boy...Samuel. And she returned him to you after he was weaned just as she vowed. But I'm not Hannah, Father. I'm Anne in the here and now, pleading with you to hear my cry for a baby. Oh, please, have mercy. My arms are empty. I'm dying of grief. If you'll give me a little boy, I'll bring him up consecrated the way Hannah brought up Samuel. I vow this before you, Mighty God. I vow!"*

TERRY WARD TUCKER

— *Anne* —

Yes, I was the distraught woman discovered by Berta and Pastor Seabrook in *New Light*'s sanctuary, dysfunctional Anne York, though I do not like admitting that now. No one who knew me back then would ever have guessed I'd fall apart in such a way. Not the fabulous Dr. York, most sought-after OB-GYN in Savannah, strongest of the strong in the female gender, never the type you would find crushed by despair late at night in a dark church. And yet...

I am sure my emotional behavior on this odd occasion has set up questions in your mind. Let's take a moment, just the two of us, to communicate frankly. I hope you will not object to my carving time out along the way to talk with you one-on-one about what caused my breakdown. I want to convey the details as clearly as I can, though they still hurt me to the core. By hurt, I don't mean owning up to the fact I was the pitiful, forlorn, miserable individual Berta and Pastor Seabrook came upon in the sanctuary, nor that I put in writing such a distraught vow to God. My ego...yes, my own huge *self* hates revealing weakness of any sort. Though I know if I do not let you in all the way, you won't be able to understand the depth of my anguish.

My problem was I wanted a baby, needed a baby. Indeed, I had come close to losing my mind over needing a baby... *but I could not get pregnant!* Though not until I failed utterly at solving the problem on my own, did I look in God's direction for help, and only then as a last resort. My pathetic, candlelit prayer vigil that you observed inside *New Light* was my lowest point, although not because of the agony of my barren state, which anyone would assume was the case. No, my lowest point was thinking I could manipulate God into giving me what I wanted. Arrogant, huh!

You were right to feel uneasy when you came upon my spent body on those altar steps, for you were in the presence of a woman who believed she could turn a deaf ear to the unselfish teachings of Jesus and negotiate on equal footing with Holy God...as if she had anything of value with which to barter that was not already his.

> [Jesus] *"You have also heard that our ancestors were told, 'You must not break your vows; you must carry out the vows you make to the Lord.' But I say, do not make any vows! Do not say, 'By heaven!' because heaven is God's throne. And do not say, 'By the earth!' because the earth is his footstool. And do not say, 'By Jerusalem!' for Jerusalem is the city of the great King. Do not even say, 'By my head!' for you can't turn one hair white or black. Just say a simple, 'Yes, I will,' or 'No, I won't.' Anything beyond this is from the evil one."*
> MATTHEW 5:33-36 NLT

Chapter

2

Four Years Earlier:

Nick and Sallie York learned early in their marriage how to throw a crazy-fun lawn party, even without alcohol as the main draw. The sociable couple had been "having a few people over for dinner" on a regular basis since their three, now-grown daughters - Anne, Rose, and Charlotte - were in diapers.

The York family estate on romantic Moon River Inlet - that wide curve off Savannah River twenty minutes east of the historic town of the same name - with its massive backyard shaded by two dozen grand oaks draped in Spanish moss, provided the perfect setting for entertaining of the laid-back variety.

On this late afternoon, folks of all ages and ethnic origins, plus a swarm of rambunctious children, milled about under Nick and Sallie's canopy of two-hundred-year-old trees, laughing and talking, enjoying the raucous music of the Frog Giggers, a local band versatile in tunes from rock to blue grass to Cajun.

A massive banner reading - CONGRATULATIONS, DR. ANNE YORK, OB-GYN - fluttered from the overhang of a temporary bandstand set up near the long dock. No one seemed to mind that the musicians were relying too heavily on a pitchy female vocalist better known as the favorite waitress at Moon River Bar and Grill.

Rose, eldest of the three York sisters, stood at the edge of the crowd, a baby girl glued to her hip. Rose observed the festivities with a certain moodiness in her eyes that over the years had become their only expression. Anyone could see she was at the party physically, but in no way participating in the joy of the occasion. She became even more glum when her younger, more attractive sister, Charlotte, strode up and delivered a message with a tone. "Mom sent me to tell you to stop pouting and start mingling, Rosie, dearest. It's not every day a York girl becomes a board certified medical doctor. The two of us barely made it through nail-art manicure training. Where is Anne, anyhow?"

Rose's bad attitude soured worse. "Somewhere showing off, no doubt," she said with a tone of her own, "accepting the Lifetime Achievement Award for Wonderfulness, our brilliant baby sister, amazing Anne."

Charlotte had no time for her older sibling's sarcasm. "Pull in your claws, Rosie. Mom's got a guy she wants Anne to meet. Husband material." She glanced at her smartwatch. "And we have to start herding this crowd into the dinner tent soon."

Rose smirked and made no move to join the search. The middle York sister, Charlotte, growled and air-clawed at Rose with all ten of her poppy red fingernails. "I'm telling Mama on you," she said. "And if you see Daddy, she's looking for him, too."

Charlotte hurried off, stretching her neck this way and

that as she resumed her quest for Anne among the giddy party guests. Rose continued nursing her own bad temper as she watched her pretty sister bounce away.

⤛⤛⤛

It made no difference to spark-plug Anne that a party in her honor was playing out in the York backyard. Proving her expertise as a slalom water skier to the passengers in her dad's motor boat was more fun than making small talk with his old cronies on the lawn. And why would she need two skis to plow up the blue-gray waters of the inlet when one would do just as well?

Anne put on her best stage smile as she gave a thumbs up to the crowd of bathing-suit-clad young men and women occupying her father's boat. They cheered her on like silly teenagers, which they were not, as she cut back and forth across the wake, waving and flirting with riders in other boats that zipped alongside her dad's Nautique.

Nick York, Anne's father and boat pilot, knew something about timing. Seconds before his daughter's audience lost interest in her slalom performance, he headed his beloved boat, *Moon Maiden*, toward the floating dock off his backyard. All Nick's passengers had been whooping and hollering when he'd changed directions by thirty degrees portside and started for home, which was the reason they did not notice. Nick stifled a grin. He knew that when the revelers realized their joyride was over, they would switch from stroking Anne's ego, to begging her gray-haired father, Nick himself, for ten more minutes on the water, which every one of them did right on cue. As Nick eased *Moon Maiden* dockside, his face

19

shone with satisfaction at making the perfect call.

He killed the motor and glanced back at Anne to make sure she was safe, watching with fatherly pride as she sank into the water and slipped her feet out of the rubber ski booties. Nick knew that his stunning daughter would not have to float alone more than a few seconds in her life vest. Two of the male boat passengers nearly came to blows over which one was going to pull her in by the ski rope.

Charlotte, now on the dock, stood frowning and tapping her foot. She did not speak for the short time it took Anne to reach the ladder, knowing it would be impossible at that distance to be heard above the Frog Giggers. But when her baby sister reached the dock via the rope, Charlotte let loose a flurry of words that would have made Sallie York, her bossy mother, quite proud. "Get up here right now, Anne. Mom's had me trying to track you down for an hour. You, too, Daddy. Sun's setting. Time to feed this horde of Philistines."

Guilty-faced passengers clambered out of *Moon Maiden* in twos and threes as Anne climbed the dock ladder. Nick addressed his middle daughter as he tied off the boat. "Why didn't your mama call out the Coast Guard like she usually does? They know her by name over there."

Charlotte ignored Nick. Her more pressing problem at the moment was dealing with the bevy of young women disembarking the boat. "Y'all's clothes better be in the boathouse," she said to the windblown social club. "All three of Mama's *Bible* classes are here. No skirtinies allowed. Daddy, where's your bow tie?"

Except for Anne, the gaggle of young women slunk toward the boathouse to change clothes. Nick pulled his wrinkled bow tie out of his pants pocket and held it up for Charlotte's approval. Anne swallowed a giggle. Said she to her ruffled sister, "My stuff is in that pile over there next to the cooler. Not much...just my cap and gown from graduation."

Charlotte kicked the rope aside and snatched up Anne's elaborate academic regalia reserved for medical doctors. The special tam fell into the water and floated away, its gold tassel bright against the cap's black velvet. Charlotte shook out the damp gown in disgust as she barked at the water-logged new graduate. "Did you undress in front of everybody on the lawn? Pastor Seabrook is up there. What's the matter with you?"

Anne feigned remorse. "I didn't get down to nothing. Had my bathing suit on underneath. I planned to flash y'all when the dean awarded me my diploma. Thought better of it at the last minute. Didn't want Mama and Daddy to have to move away."

Nick chortled, but said nothing. He was busy retying his bow tie using the boat's rear view mirror.

Charlotte stomped toward the boathouse, destination of the other young women. She accosted the last one in line and held up the academic gown as a threat. "You can either wear this, Bonnie Lynn, or stay down here on the dock for the rest of the party. Choose your poison."

Bonnie Lynn made a face at Charlotte at the same time trading her strapless dress for the gown. Charlotte rushed back to Anne, who by then was wringing water out of her hair. She watched her sister grab a beach towel off *Moon Maiden* and thrust it, along with Bonnie Lynn's dress, toward two of the male boaters. "Here," she said to the surprised compadres. "Make a curtain for Anne to change behind. And don't look at her, or I'll tell every one of your wives where you've been. Anne, did you wear shoes down here?"

"In the boat," Anne yelled from behind the towel curtain.

Charlotte retrieved her sister's wet high heels, all the while glaring at the untrustworthy towel holders. Anne made another announcement from behind the curtain. "Guess I'll have to go without undies. Got nothing but this wet bathing suit."

One of the fellows whistled through his teeth. Charlotte stared him into silence. "On that note," said Nick, "I think I'll mosey on back to the party before Sallie serves me with divorce papers."

Charlotte shooed Nick up the dock toward the lawn and handed Anne her stilettos over the towel. She said to her wayward sister, "Forget panties. Mom's pitching a hissy fit to start dinner. She wants to give you your graduation gift in front of everybody. You know Mama...got to have an audience."

Anne held onto a forearm of one of the male towel holders while slipping on her shoes. "Ready, boys?" she shouted. "Drop the curtain!"

The young men let the towel fall to the dock, revealing a smiling Anne in exaggerated cheerleader pose. Bonnie Lynn's strapless dress never looked better. Anne's male audience clapped and cheered. She laughed and bear-hugged Charlotte. Said the carefree Anne to her annoyed sister, "Come along, dear kinswoman of mine. Let us make our way to the festival and walk amongst the little people."

— Anne —

Here I am, yet again. Can you believe how full of myself I was back then, showing off like a prima donna on one ski behind Daddy's boat? Pride personified. Not that Dad saw me that way. His biased opinion was simple - his youngest daughter could not help being born with a whopping dose of personality. "When Anne walks into a room," he'd brag to anyone who would listen, "the sub-atomic particles in the air start spinning in opposite directions."

I loved that he considered me his most confident daughter, happy go lucky Annie, polar opposite to Rose, oldest and most serious of the three York sisters. Rose was so jealous of me that her face glowed radioactive green on most days, not that I cared. My middle sister, Charlotte, thought I was fabulous. So did Mom. And I guess I was at the time...in a worldly sort of way. I had no spiritual sensibilities whatsoever, nor eternal. But what did that matter? Spiritual and eternal things held no importance to a heart like mine, all swollen to bursting with pride in *self*. Neither did God. I had no need of him, not when I was busy leading a charmed life, or so everyone thought, including me. Oh, I was full of myself all right, when I should have been full of Jesus.

> [Paul] *In your relationships with one another, have the same mindset of Christ Jesus: Who, being in very nature God, did not consider equality with God something to be used to his own advantage; rather, he made himself nothing by taking the very nature of a servant, being made in human likeness. And being found in appearance as a man, he humbled himself by becoming obedient to death, even death on a cross!*
> **PHILIPPIANS 2:5-8 NIV**

Chapter

After moonlight had turned the inlet waters from purple to silver, a massive party tent with open sides and dramatic lighting provided the perfect venue for Anne's graduation dinner. The Frog Giggers remained outside on the open-air bandstand just close enough to the tent to provide atmosphere music, their rendition of "Blue Bayou" the most beautiful ballad in their repertoire.

According to Nick York, no extravagance was too great for Anne. Eleven York family members sat at a horseshoe-shaped head table elevated on a wooden platform a foot above the guest tables. When dessert time rolled around, Nick stood and clinked his glass with a spoon. Everyone went quiet.

"Hope y'all enjoyed that expensive tenderloin," he said into a handheld microphone. "Sallie cleaned out my wallet putting it on the menu." Laughter rippled across the crowd. "Hey," Nick continued, "it's not every day a daughter graduates from medical school a second time. Me and my newly empty bank account now know that a doctor has to go to med school extra years to reach OB-GYN status. Though I do have one question for you, Annie. How come I'm the guy who had to bankroll all that education? Why didn't you take out loans like the rest of those clowns up there getting sheepskins today?"

Anne, hair still damp from skiing, jumped to her feet on the pretense of being insulted. She had no need of a mike. "Nick York, are you going to tell these nice people our deal, or am I?"

Nick gestured, giving her the floor, which she took with relish. "The *truth* is this old man told me he would pay my way through medical school if I'd promise to take care of him and Mama in their dotage...me seeing to their medical needs; Rosie, the cooking and housework; and Charlotte, the praying."

More gentle laughter floated up from the tables. Charlotte, seated next to Anne, stood up and spoke louder than her sister. "And I'm starting my part of the bargain right now. You fellows down there passing out those dessert plates...wait a minute while I say another blessing." She squeezed her eyes shut and clasped her hands together. "Dear, Lord, thank you for family, friends, food, and fellowship. And thank you for Anne's newest accomplishment. Bless everything to your service and glory. In Jesus' name, amen."

As Charlotte waved the dessert waiters back into action, her mother, Sallie, stood again and took the microphone from her husband. "Charlotte," Sallie said, "you and Anne sit down. You, too, Nick. I've got a few words of my own to say. First, congratulations to our newest graduate."

Sallie applauded Anne, intimidating a few guests to applaud with her. Anne crossed her hands over her heart in gratitude to her mother. Sallie smiled and went on with her speech. "And a loving nod to Charlotte for thanking God for our blessings like she always does." Charlotte made praying hands and blew a kiss to her mom, who, from the look on her face, was growing pleased with the sound of her own voice in the mike. "And a special thanks to Rosie for organizing this celebration in a manner that has bankrupted her daddy for the rest of his natural life."

More laughter erupted from the captive audience. Rose pasted on a weak smile and nodded toward her mother, after which she returned instantly to her unpleasant expression. Sallie continued forcing her bored guests to pay homage to the York family. "And, finally, my deepest gratitude to the rest of our in-laws, out-laws, and grandchildren up here at the head table, and every one of you out there at the guest tables. You are all our dear loved ones. Rosie, do you have anything to add?"

Rose knew better than to share her true feelings about the evening. "No, Mama. I'm good," she said.

Sallie smiled approval at Rose before addressing her middle daughter. "How about you, Charlotte?"

Charlotte also waved a no, whereupon Sallie rounded off her list of children with Anne. "You, Annie? Anything?"

"Couldn't have done it without you, Mama. You, either, Daddy."

Sallie dabbed at her eyes with a linen napkin. "Oh, honey, we love you so much...couldn't be more proud." The aging York matriarch then took a theatrical moment to compose herself before continuing. "Our dear Lord has blessed us so extravagantly," she said, a quaver in her voice. "I guess that's about it for the York clan patting each other on the back, except for the presentation of a little graduation gift to Anne from her daddy and me. Enjoy your desserts, everybody.

Dance until dawn!"

Nick took an envelope from his jacket pocket and handed it to Sallie, who held it up for Anne to come and collect. "Congratulations, sweetheart," she said yet again.

Folks nearest the platform applauded a last weary time. Anne went through the proper, if empty, motions of gratitude as she got up and accepted the envelope from her mother. Everyone seemed relieved when she made her way back to her seat next to Charlotte, and more so when the Frog Giggers resumed sawing away on their flat rendition of "I Had the Time of My Life." At long last, the bored guests returned to their small talk and desserts.

Anne huddled closer to Charlotte and stage whispered, "Yep, dance until dawn with no booze to make you think you can."

"Hush," Charlotte said. "Mom might hear. You'll hurt her feelings."

Anne brushed off Charlotte's concern. "Here," she said. "Put this envelope in your purse with all that makeup junk you carry around. Nothing in it, anyway...just a prop for Mama's show time. Daddy signed the legal paperwork for my new office last week. Hammered out the details over lunch at his attorney's golf club. Beats going downtown to a depressing law firm to do bi'ness."

Anne paused and stared across the horseshoe at her sister, Rose. "Look at Rosie over there. Who licked the red off her candy this time?"

Rose and her husband, William, sat midway in the opposite row, ignoring each other and everybody else. Rose busied herself helping their children with pie and ice cream, while William concentrated on his own dessert plate.

Charlotte's husband, Thomas, seated on the other side of Charlotte from Anne, was the mirror image of William across the horseshoe. He, like William, had eyes for nothing but the massive wedge of bourbon pecan pie a la mode the waiter had just placed before him. Neither fellow, Thomas nor William, who happened to be twin brothers, could have cared less about the antics of their wives and sisters-in-law. After all, Rose, Charlotte, and Anne were always cat fighting. As their father, Nick, would say, "Those girls of mine go at it louder than the Frog Giggers and more off key."

Anne and Charlotte stared in curious silence as their oldest sister, Rose, multi-tasked among her brood of chicks. After careful study, Charlotte said, "I know what her problem is. She's sick on her stomach from being pregnant again. Four babies one after the other must not make nausea any easier."

Anne fake smiled and waved to Rose, who fake smiled and waved back. Charlotte did not participate in this charade. She had a news flash of her own. "I'm pregnant, too," she told Anne, giving her a punch in the shoulder. "How about that!"

Anne made a wow face. "What? You and Thomas haven't been married a month."

Anne leaned around Charlotte toward Thomas. "Is this true, Tom?" she said. "You're going to be a daddy?"

"Afraid so. Took a minimum of skill."

Charlotte disregarded Thomas' cliché. "We've been married six months, not one," she said to Anne. "And I'm naming the baby after you."

"How do you know it's a girl?"

Charlotte patted her own belly. "Too early for an ultrasound, but since Rosie can't give birth to anything but future members of the Savannah Junior League, I don't hold out much boy-hope for myself. It'll be a girl...Annie, the second."

"Better be," Anne said. "I intend to have the first boy around here."

"You plan to get a husband first?"

"Left up to me, no. Who's that dude at Table Three down there, next to Bonnie Lynn? Keeps trying to catch my eye."

"Her cousin from Alabama. Moved here last month to work for Jet Aircraft. He's the one Mama wanted you to meet before you went A-WOL on the inlet. Gabe Simmons."

Anne sipped her iced tea and made eye contact with the young man, who smiled at her. She leaned forward and waved a single pinkie at him. "Guess he'll have to do then," she said to Charlotte. "If I drag some fringy guy of my own choosing up in here, Mama and Daddy'll have to leave Savannah." She went thoughtful as she studied Gabe Simmons' open face. Shrugging, she said, "Seems nice enough. Hope he doesn't put up a fuss about me keeping York as my last name."

— *Anne* —

It's me again – the newly *un*fabulous Anne - this time to acknowledge a bit of humiliation. It isn't easy allowing you to see how full of pride and self-sufficiency I was back then. Rose considered me obnoxious, unfair on her part, unless you agree that obnoxious equates with success. I think it was Rose's way of dealing with envy. My side of the story goes like this: Just because I was able to make difficult accomplishments look easy did not mean they were. For example, I worked so hard at becoming an OB-GYN that on most days I thought I might collapse from sheer exhaustion. But Rose never witnessed those grim times. She did not know they were part and parcel of my physical and emotional landscape. Not that I wanted her to. Nor did I want her help. Why would I? I could achieve anything on perseverance alone, to include becoming a medical doctor with difficult specialties like obstetrics and gynecology. I called my independent model for success Never-Give-Up-No-Matter-What, which defined my history. It was the secret to all my triumphs. Okay, I concede that Daddy always made sure I lived within his financial safety net, but he could not do my academic work. In that arena, I was on my own. And though I admit to struggling occasionally, most of the time I excelled. So then, with Dad's support and my own strong will, you can see why I had bright expectations for my future.

I had good reason to be proud of all I had achieved, as did Daddy, although we were both prouder of my ability to face down hardships associated with working toward difficult goals rather than merely completing them. I went so far as to make boisterous pride an integral part of my personality, a trait some folks close to me, though not all, found fun and exciting. Rose didn't, for certain. Never mind she had pride issues of her own, of a lackluster variety to be sure, but as dense with arrogance as mine, more so when you throw in self-righteousness, conceit, jealousy, and resentment, which accounts for the extra dashes of sinful yeast in her bitter personality. But who am I to judge my oldest sister? I am no one and nothing, never have been, not even when I thought I was...especially when I thought I was. For without Jesus, that is who we all are, chaff in the wind destined for the searing fire.

For you say, I am rich, I have prospered,
and I need nothing, not realizing that you are
wretched, pitiable, poor, blind, and naked.
REVELATION 3:17 ESV

Clothe yourselves, all of you, with humility toward
one another, for "God opposes the proud but
gives grace to the humble."
1 PETER 5:5B ESV

[Jesus] *Do not judge, or you too will be judged.*
MATTHEW 7:1 NIV

[Jesus] *His winnowing fork is in his hand to clear his*
threshing floor and to gather the wheat into his barn, but he
will burn up the chaff with unquenchable fire.
LUKE 3:17 NIV

Chapter

4

Dr. York – Anne – remained perfectly still as she listened to her pregnant patient's abdomen through her stethoscope. Leslie, the young African American woman lying flat on Anne's examination table, held her breath and waited for the doctor's verdict. Anne smiled and draped the stethoscope around her neck. "Your baby's ticker is stronger than a pony's, Leslie. Let me help you up."

Anne covered Leslie's belly with a sheet and pulled her to a seated position on the side of the table. Leslie grimaced. She rested a hand on her round belly. "Oh...ow," she said. "Kicks like a pony, too." She waited a moment for her baby to settle down. "Dr. York, my mom told me to ask about your daddy. Is he any better?"

Anne answered without taking her eyes off her laptop screen. "Not the man he used to be. Chemo has sapped his strength."

"And your mother is still trying to take care of him at home, right?"

"Yes, with visiting health care services...and my sisters and me helping out."

Leslie looked sad. She watched Anne's fingers tap, tap, tapping on the computer keyboard as she entered information from the exam. "Have you thought about calling in hospice?" Leslie said, concern in her voice.

"No, no. He's not that bad...just convalescing from treatments right now."

"I'll tell Mom," said the girl. "She and Dad dragged me to both your medical school graduations. Wedding, too. They wanted me to see what a young woman succeeding in life looked like...a role model." She paused. "What's that been, four years now?"

Anne closed her laptop and faced Leslie. "Three since the wedding. Four, the last graduation. I remember your being there, not long before..."

"Yes," Leslie said, "before my own dad died. He loved your mother. Got the biggest kick out of telling how Sallie York would grab both your hands and pray for you right out loud in the produce section of Food King. That was my daddy."

"That's still my mama."

Leslie gazed into Anne's eyes, enjoying what she mistook as attention from a personal friend. She found out otherwise on getting too familiar. "Doesn't seem right," she said, "a girl as young as me having a baby before you."

Anne picked up her laptop from the counter and headed for the door. "You and your little one are both doing great, Les. I almost said give my love to your dad. Old habits die hard. See you in a few weeks...your regular check-up."

Anne, the competent and cool-headed young doctor, clicked the door shut behind her with finality, ending Leslie's interrogation in addition to her medical visit. Leslie thought to speak again, but what was there to say to a closed door?

❦

Anne sat at her father's bedside and watched him sleep. After a few moments, Rose came into the sick room, carrying Nick's covered dinner tray. Anne cleared a space for it on the bedside table, at the same time speaking to her sister. "I don't mind helping Daddy with his supper tonight, Rose, if you've got something else to do."

Rose's face flushed. "That's the way it always is with you," she said, her voice shaky. "Let somebody else do the grunt work while you walk away with the showy part."

"Will you stop? I can't take your hostility when Dad's so down."

Nick opened his eyes. He focused on Rose, his eldest. "Go get your mother, Rosie. I want her to help me."

Rose gave Anne a dirty look before leaving. Anne imitated her sister's grouchy face, then she turned and smirked at Nick, who smirked back. "Rosie thinks I favor you," he said.

"She's right. You do."

"Not really, just looks that way. You were my last shot at producing a boy. Thank God in his infinite wisdom I didn't succeed. No boy could have measured up to the likes of you."

Anne peeked under the cover of the dinner tray. "Yum, apple pie. Want to have your dessert first?"

"I'll let your mother decide. By the way, did you know Rose will be thirty-eight next month? She's mighty young to have five daughters already. Her newest little scamp is a real cutie. I thought four would be enough for Rose, but along came number five."

"I wondered who that new kid was at Sunday dinner last week. Yep, Rose's only talent is spitting out babies."

Anne's attempt to cheer her father fell flat. He refused to be redirected. "Do you think Charlotte would have had more children," he said, "if Little Annie hadn't been born with Down's? I can't help wondering, what with Rose having so many healthy babies. They show up on roller skates over at her house."

"Come on, Dad. You know Rose never misses an opportunity to parade her progeny before the family, especially me, childless. She's an Olympian gold medalist in the sport of procreation. And she torments Charlotte, too, who can't help it her health is iffy, one kidney and it weak, and Thomas leaving like he did after Little Annie was born with Down's. Why do you want to pour salt on my and Charlotte's wounds?"

"Thought I was being subtle. Missed the mark, I guess."

Anne cocked her head like a spaniel. "By a country mile."

Her father dug his hole deeper. "I was counting up y'all's ages this morning. Didn't have anything else to do. And I realized my youngest, you, hit thirty-three this year. Are you and Gabe part of that new modern crowd against having children?"

Sallie bustled into the bedroom and began the process of getting Nick ready for his meal. She saved Anne from having to answer Nick's question. "Are you nagging at Anne again, Nick York? You never can let a thing just lie there. Been trying to make a boy out of the poor girl since the day she was born."

Anne mimicked Sallie's bossiness. "Yeah, since the day I was born."

Sallie ignored Anne's remark and kept talking. "And after she's done everything in the world to please you. Medical school...twice! A successful OB-GYN practice. Marriage. Nice house. Fine cars. What more could you ask of one little girl?"

Anne nodded. "Yeah, what more could you ask of one little girl?"

Sallie popped the towel she was about to spread across Nick's pajama top. "Stop with your sassy talk," she said to Anne. "Go help Rose finish cleaning the kitchen. She's exhausted from hosting her book club meeting this afternoon, on top of the baby's got a fever."

Anne slipped on her jacket and grabbed her purse. "Cleaning the kitchen is women's work," she said. "I have to go home and make sure Gabe cleaned ours."

Her mother shoved a bite of creamed corn into Nick's mouth, at the same time reprimanding Anne. "You know I don't appreciate smart-mouth, young lady. That's for your father to put up with. Now get your over-educated self in the kitchen and help your sister."

Anne slumped her shoulders in mock surrender and moped toward the bedroom door. She acknowledged her father on leaving, but not her mother. "Bye, Daddy. Really nice visiting with you today, discussing my biological time clock and all. Maybe tomorrow we can talk about my irregularity."

Sallie pointed with the fork toward the open door. Anne

departed with a laugh. Nick picked up the spoon from his tray and began eating on his own, though he soon grew too weary to continue. Sallie took over and made it a point to keep the momentum of his dinner going. She was a good nurse. She knew what her patient needed.

Nick talked between bites. "Anne turned thirty-three this year, Sal, with no sign of a chap."

Sallie speared a potato wedge and offered it to her tired husband, who nibbled around its edges without enjoyment. "And you turned seventy-two," she said, "with chaps and grandchaps to spare."

Sallie was about to say more, but Anne's voice from downstairs interrupted her. "Bye, Mama, Daddy, Rosie," she yelled. "Sorry I didn't have time to help in the kitchen."

— *Anne* —

Interesting, is it not, the intense need I had to ratchet up the appearance in Daddy's eyes of being in control of my life, when the opposite was true. I had encountered the terrible problem of infertility, which my heart interpreted as a personal failure. You can imagine how frustrated I felt. Was it not enough to be tormented privately by my inability to get pregnant? Why did I have to endure the cruel, unwritten requirement that eventually my suffering would be made public? Dad and my pregnant patient, Leslie, would have been shocked to learn how their questions had wounded me on the morning and afternoon of the same day. Don't get me wrong. I was not angry at either one of those kind people. I knew their hearts were in the right places. I was furious, however, at my own inability to cope with their innocent curiosity. Neither Dad nor Leslie, nor anyone else for that matter, had the remotest idea of how long I had been struggling with my affliction. Strong word, affliction. Nevertheless, that is how I ranked my condition. I felt afflicted in the worst possible way. Slow torture. Slow failure. Sharp pain. Dull pain. Every kind of pain imaginable for weeks and more weeks, months and more months. For the cold reality of my infertility did not come at me in a rush. It broke my heart an inch at a time. At first, I was able to hang onto hope and confidence without falling apart every twenty-eight days. Things will work out, I told myself at the end of each monthly cycle when nothing happened. As an OB-GYN, I knew Mother Nature often took her own sweet time in such matters. I had grown accustomed to reassuring my patients about this fact of life. But now here I was, trying with less conviction to reassure myself. As months rolled by with no baby, my natural confidence began giving way to anxiety, a state of mind unfamiliar and disconcerting to me. I began worrying in secret. Questions with no answers tugged at my heart. What should I do to address my problem? How long should I wait before getting checked out medically? For the first time in my life, I felt unsure of myself, though pride kept me from sharing my heartache, not even with Gabe at first. How could I admit something was going wrong in my fairy tale life, especially something I had assumed would be effortless and on a schedule of my own choosing? I countered worry and confusion by ramping up my signature, carefree attitude, which rang more hollow with every passing day. Behind my façade, I brooded alone in quiet distress about what steps I should take next. And not just brood, I worried myself sick. And not just sick, but desperate as I slid down a spiral of frayed nerves and increasing exhaustion. For the first time in my life, I felt out of control.

Do not be anxious about anything, but in every situation,
by prayer and petition, with thanksgiving, present your
requests to God. And the peace of God, which transcends
all understanding, will guard your hearts
and your minds in Christ Jesus.
PHILIPPIANS 4:6-7 NIV

Chapter

Downstairs in Sallie York's kitchen, Rose made more noise than was necessary loading her mother's dishwasher. When finished, she pressed the start button with emphasis and began wiping down the counter tops, microwave, stove, and sink. As she started on the refrigerator, Sallie came into the kitchen bearing Nick's dinner tray, his plate only partially empty.

"Oh, sweetheart," Sallie said to Rose. She set the tray down by the sink and wiped perspiration from her brow with her apron. "Thank you for cleaning up. Sometimes I get so tired I can hardly go. My strength is failing me in my old age. Your daddy fell asleep in the middle of his apple pie. Can't say I wasn't glad."

Rose gave the fridge a last swipe, then she moved to the sink to rinse her father's dinner dishes. Sallie touched her daughter's arm. "Time to take a break, dear," she said. "You've done enough for one day. Let's go outside...breathe some fresh air, get our minds off things."

Rose looked her mother straight in the eye. "What things, Mom? It's the same as always around here, except for Daddy getting weaker by the day."

Sallie took the wet dishtowel from Rose and tossed it onto the counter top. "I'm still your mama, Rosie. I know when something is on your mind."

Rose stared down at her own white knuckles and said nothing. Sallie took off her apron and laid it next to the dishtowel. She pulled her daughter toward the back door, cajoling her as they bumbled along together. "Come see the garden. Daddy's Wineberry Candy Lilies look like orchids this year. They make me feel better every time I visit them."

Sallie donned gloves and a straw hat in the garage before continuing on to the garden with Rose. Hedge clippers in hand, she smiled at the dozens of new blossoms. "Oh, Rose... Rosie, look how beautiful they are. How could they possibly be real? Reminds me of what Jesus said in *Matthew 6:28-29*. *'And why take ye thought for raiment? Consider the lilies of the field, how they grow; they toil not, neither do they spin. And yet I say unto you, that even Solomon in all his glory was not arrayed like one of these.'* "

She held up a single lily and smiled at her daughter, whose face was drawn with fatigue. Sallie's cheerful countenance turned stern. "Out with it, Rose," she said. "It'll fester if you keep it bottled up."

Rose's irritation grew more brittle. "You already know, Mom."

Sallie nodded. "Yes, I do, but you'll feel better if you say it out loud to someone who loves you, who won't judge."

Rose dropped the basket to the flagstones, scattering her mother's cut lilies. She wheeled around and headed for the yard chairs nearby, sinking into the nearest one, covering her face with her hands. Sallie took off her gloves and followed

Rose. She sat down next to her moody daughter and let the gloves fall to the grass. "Just say it, darling. No one else is here."

Rose let out a shuddering sigh. "It's Anne, always Anne. And Daddy...the way he carries on about her. I have five perfect daughters, and Charlotte has Little Annie...precious even if she is challenged. But Daddy still does nothing but fall all over Anne, sympathizing with her about her childlessness, going on about how superior she is, raising her higher on that pedestal he keeps her on. I feel like gagging every time I hear it."

Rose dropped her head again and paused a moment, her shoulders rounded and bent. Sallie stroked her child's back, which, instead of calming Rose, agitated her into spewing out more venom. "Oh, yes," she said, straightening her torso with a jerk, "the wonderful Anne York goes around pretending she doesn't care about having children, but you and I both know she'd give her eyeteeth to have the only boy...for daddy...but really for more attention. Don't deny it, Mom."

It was Sallie's turn to sigh. "I can't deny what's true, Rosie...about Anne...and your father. You aren't the only one hurt by that old man's insensitivity. How do you think I've felt all these years? I'm his wife, supposed to be first in his life...after God, of course. But when I couldn't give him the son he wanted, and Anne was born a girl, and then I wasn't able to have more children..."

"Stop it, Mom. You're breaking my heart. I never thought about it like that. I've been too focused on Anne, the prodigal daughter, and how she and Daddy have always affected Charlotte and me. We're nothing but the boring, loyal sisters who stayed home to serve the family."

Sallie tightened her brow into deep creases. "I don't understand," she said. "Anne hasn't ever run off anyplace."

Rose stiffened her back in frustration. "How can you not see the obvious, Mom? Anne has run off in the worst way possible. Not physically...Spiritually! She believes in herself, not Jesus or God or the Holy Spirit. She has rejected every important thing you and Daddy ever tried to teach her. But not the blessings. Oh, no, never those...still gobbles them up like the greedy pig she's always been. And the more Daddy pours on her, the more she grabs."

"Rose...Rosie, what's gotten into you? I can't let you speak so harshly about your sister. Your father is generous to all three of you girls."

"Yes, Mom, he is, but there's a difference you won't acknowledge. Charlotte and I are grateful, mindful, thankful. And we always try to give back. But Anne considers herself entitled. She doesn't give back anything. And the most ridiculous part is that one day, as predictable as rain, she'll make a big, showy splash of coming home again...Spiritually, I mean, and expect to be congratulated even for that. Can't you see how thrilled Daddy will be over her fake repentance? Throw a party. Kill the fatted calf. And if she ever manages to have a baby, a boy, to throw on top of all her other accomplishments, heaven itself won't hold her. Never mind that Charlotte and I have always been faithful and loyal and respectful to you and daddy both. But when the favored youngest daughter changes her ways, nothing Charlotte and I have ever done will be remembered. Anne has spent her whole adult life disrespecting everything and everybody, even

God. When was the last time you saw her in church with Gabe and the rest of us...her family? She's the prodigal daughter all right. I can't believe Charlotte hasn't wised up. She's nothing to Anne but another admirer."

"Oh, my dear...my poor, poor Rose. Where has your forgiveness gone? You know Daddy loves you and Charlotte as much as he loves Anne."

Rose regarded her mother with pity. "Does he, Mom? The truth is...he doesn't love you as much."

TERRY WARD TUCKER

— *Anne* —

Believe me - and this is the unvarnished truth - if I had understood the depth of Rose's resentment toward me, and my own part in fueling it, I would have jumped off the nearest cliff. My unkind reason for not behaving more responsibly toward my oldest sister was my preoccupation with self's desires. You know the drill. Poor me, poor me, all about me! And you are also aware of the blinding fixation that had overtaken my life, the need to do everything I could to get pregnant. I'm being easy on myself referring to my problem as a simple fixation, when any observer could have identified my behavior as evidence of a full-blown psychotic obsession.

Rose did not have it in her experience to comprehend what I was going through. How could she? She had already given birth to five healthy daughters. We were light years apart in relating. I think it would be fair to say two sisters could not have understood each other less. Can you believe I thought Rose gave birth to five children just to impress everyone with her wonderfulness as a mother? And just as dysfunctional, can you believe Rose had somehow convinced herself I went to medical school and specialized in obstetrics and gynecology for the sole purpose of showcasing myself as superior to those around me? Our mom must have thanked God every day for Charlotte, her only daughter with a pure heart. Rose and I were too busy finding fault with each other to bother cultivating virtues like purity. It is difficult even now to disclose how much unhealthy gratification I derived from knowing Rose was envious of me. And we were both wrong to get into the habit of attacking each other's motives for personal decisions. Wrong, petty, and childish. Sadly, our cycle of negativity was harder on Rose than on me. She allowed my transgressions to eat at her, while I barely noticed hers.

Poor Rose. I drove her crazy back then. And so did Daddy, though he never tormented her for sport the way I did on occasion. On that score, he was as innocent as I was guilty. Which Rose knew with as much certainty as she knew how much I wanted a baby. You must agree, she was insensitive relative to my childlessness. Not that I hold it against her now. I've let all that go, which was easier than letting my own offenses go. I still feel guilty whenever I look back on how miserable Rose's life had become. And I think I'm probably correct in blaming myself for much of her distress. Why couldn't I have been more understanding, forgiving, even loving toward my sister in a genuine, Godly way? And why couldn't my sister have had a more tender heart as she watched me endure the pain of infertility? Though the real kicker was that my and Rose's relationship was not the only rocky one in our family. Gabe and I were not the perfect couple. Sometimes now, with the clarity of hindsight, I wonder why I could not see that my escalating problems with those close to me had a single fundamental cause - my own pride. Why did I not humble myself before God, open my *Bible*, read, study, or pray? Most of all, why did I wait so long to begin praying that my life, and the lives of everyone around me, would be healed in Jesus by the power of the Spirit? Why? Why? Why?

> But Jesus called them unto him, and said, Ye know that
> the princes of the Gentiles exercise dominion over them,
> and they that are great exercise authority upon them. But

it shall not be so among you: but whosoever will be great among you, let him be your minister; And whosoever will be chief among you, let him be your servant: Even as the Son of man came not to be ministered unto, but to minister, and to give his life a ransom for many.
MATTHEW 20:25-28 KJV

TERRY WARD TUCKER

Chapter

Gabe slept in a lounge chair on the pool terrace, mouth open, snore function working overtime. His ten-minute break from cleaning the pool had turned into an hour-long snooze punctuated by rapid eye movements. He remained in dreamland as Anne entered the pool hardscape area through the back gate off the driveway. She walked over and stood observing him for an amused moment before waking him with a kiss and a question. "Did you clean the kitchen, Rip Van Winkle?"

Gabe sat straight up in his chair. "What...what? I get around to it once a week or so."

"Never mind. Order some Italian food while I shower. Bella Casa delivers fastest, if the police haven't locked up their grill jockey again for public intoxication."

"Yes, ma'am, Dr. York. Nothing like having Bella Casa every other night."

Anne's expression made it clear she did not care for competition in cracking wise. "Good," she said. "We'll have it every night from now on."

Anne and Gabe communed with the TV instead of each other as they ate dinner side by side on the living room sofa. They had settled on watching a documentary since the local news was long since over. Gabe appeared engrossed in the announcer's list of theories behind the dwindling population of Monarch butterflies on the East Coast. Anne made a weak effort to redirect his attention.

"I'm thirty-three now," she said. "That makes you thirty-five."

"Thirty-six in a month," Gabe said, unconcerned. "Those butterflies can't find their way back home from Mexico, the poor stiffs."

Anne nudged him with an elbow. "Gabe, we're both in our thirties."

He shrugged. "Thirties are the new twenties according to the Internet, the world's source of all truth and wisdom." He took a huge bite of baked ziti and returned to the subject of flying insects. "We used to see thousands of Monarchs in Alabama when I was a kid. Swarmed all over. It's Alabama's official state insect, you know."

"Stop talking with your mouth full. Don't you think it's time we had a baby? Babies?"

Gabe turned and stared at his wife, another forkful of pasta poised in midair. "On account of the monarchs getting lost?"

Anne picked up the remote and switched off the TV. Gabe put his fork down. Anne met his gaze as she spoke. "Look, I know you've been protecting my feelings about this.

We've been trying to have a baby for three years now without ever talking about it. And every month you pretend you don't care when it doesn't happen. You've been doing that forever to keep from hurting me. But you do care. I see how you dote on Charlotte's Annie. So...I made an appointment for us at a clinic downtown...to find out what the problem is."

Gabe set his tray on the coffee table. Anne clattered her own tray on top of it. He pulled her closer on the sofa and wrapped his arms around her shoulders. "Listen here, slugger. I care about having a baby for one reason, that I know it's important to you. But my hottie little wife – you! – would be enough for me the rest of my life with or without a baby."

"I'm not your hottie little wife. I'm your no-good wife, putting you last all these years while I built up my medical practice, acting like your needs never mattered. I wouldn't even take your last name."

"I knew you didn't love me when we got married, Anne. I just dropped into your life at a convenient moment. But I've never complained or held it against you."

"That's what I mean, what I know. You're a good egg, like Daddy. And I'm a rotten egg." She choked back tears. "Daddy wants me to have a baby before he dies, a grandson. And I haven't been able to give him one, or you, or myself. I've tried to live up to every expectation anyone ever had of me, but with this, the most important thing, I've flopped like a dying fish, worse than as a wife."

"Nick wants you to have a baby for yourself, not him. He's afraid he may have caused you to miss out on being a mother...pushing you so hard to be a York superhero, like he would have pushed a son if he'd had one. And then he got cancer, which started him thinking it had all backfired, that he might have made you wait too long and lose your shot at having a family."

"Seems like he wants a grandson awful bad." Anne sniffed and rubbed the back of her neck. Then she asked the question she had been trying to ask all evening. "Are you willing to go through the medical fertility thing with me, Gabe? Or maybe I should be calling it the infertility thing. A couple of years ago I thought you might leave altogether... vamoose."

"It crossed my mind, and you never seemed to care one way or the other. But then Nick got sick, and Rose ramped up her earth mother act...*look-Mama-and-Daddy-at-the-brood-of-amazing-grandkids-I've-produced*. I couldn't leave you to deal with that alone. Nick's cancer, either. So now you're stuck with me for good."

"Nobody in the family knows this baby thing has become an issue."

Nick laughed aloud. "Just because you haven't told them doesn't mean they don't know, Sherlock. You need to ask Charlotte and your mama to start praying."

"Our first appointment at the clinic is tomorrow morning. Can you take the day off?"

"Oh, yeah. I'm in for the long haul. Bring on the test tubes!"

Anne and Gabe sat barely breathing as Dr. Armond explained the intimidating processes and procedures that go with treating infertility. "It's not nearly as hit-or-miss as it used to be," he said, sounding for the world as if reciting a sales pitch. "These days we have an established protocol with a high success rate. Most couples who have sat in those same chairs have had a good outcome, a healthy baby. More than one in some cases."

He chuckled. Then, like a robot, he switched back to his serious demeanor and scripted speech. "Though to be honest, some have suffered serious trauma along the way, both emotional and physical, same as you two now, particularly the wives. Women who try to get pregnant a year or two with no luck...let's say they develop tendencies."

"Three," Gabe said. "We've been married three years with no baby."

Dr. Armond leaned forward in his chair. "I'll do everything I can to help you, Mr. Simmons...everything you can afford."

Gabe took Anne's hand and squeezed it. "We'll afford whatever it takes."

Anne stared at her husband's profile and wept.

— Anne —

It was not easy letting Gabe in on my new opinion of myself, an abject failure. Infertility is notorious for stealing a woman's confidence, no matter how centered and accomplished she is. I found this out in a personal way when it stole mine. Gabe showed no real surprise on the night I broke over and shared my heart with him. He was not completely in the dark, after all. I hadn't gotten pregnant over a period of time too long for normal in a woman not practicing birth control. That much he knew. What he had miscalculated, however, was the level of distress my "failure" to conceive was causing me. The tremor in my voice - when I tried to explain things to him over dinner that night in front of the TV - was the first chink he had ever seen in my armor of self-assurance, the first falter, first weakness. I was grateful for the way he reacted to my confession. His sweet insistence that he was willing to do anything and everything to help me solve my/our problem was encouraging...for a little while, anyway. I had no reason to disbelieve him. Gabe was a sincere person. But in this case, sadly, he had no idea how far anything and everything could go. Nor did I, not even with my background as an OB-GYN. Infertility was not my specialty, although I knew more about it than Gabe did. I had been studying the subject obsessively since it had become my burden. I suppose the fact I chose to keep most of what I learned to myself says something about my character. Or maybe it was the first indication my worsening emotional distress was affecting my ability to make sound decisions. Gabe did not realize I was teetering on the edge of a cliff, about to fall off and hit every jagged rock on the way down, or worse, by association, that he was about to fall with me.

Humble yourselves, therefore, under God's mighty hand, that he may lift you up in due time. Cast all your anxiety upon him because he cares for you.
1 PETER 5:6-7 NIV

Chapter

7

As always on Saturday mornings, Manuel's Lawn Service van sat tall and proud in Nick and Sallie's driveway. Anne and Gabe, dressed in rough outdoor wear, worked alongside Manuel's crew in the lower backyard near the dock. Nick sat brooding in an Adirondack on the terrace. He scowled as he watched the workers manicure his lawn. Judging from his expression, the landscapers were of far more interest than the cheerful trio of red and yellow kayaks skimming along the surface of Moon River in the distance. Nick barely noticed when his wife, Sallie, came bustling out to the terrace from the kitchen, tea tumbler in hand.

Sallie frowned and handed the tumbler to her grumpy husband. "Stop sulking," she said, wiping her hands on her apron. "You can't do yard work, anymore, and that's that."

Nick took a sip of tea, which failed at changing his mood. Anne, still at work in the lower yard, glanced toward her dad on the terrace and did not like what she saw. She propped her rake against a live oak and walked up to investigate the problem. Her father motioned her to sit next to him.

Sallie, now red in the face from exasperation, remained standing. "Maybe you can do something with him," she said to Anne. "He's forgotten how to count it all for joy."

Nick shifted in his chair, annoyed. "I counted it all for joy when I was doing my own yard work," he said, "not watching somebody else do it."

"Tell you what," Anne said. "You can come over to our house tomorrow and clean the pool."

Nick grimaced. "You can count that all for misery," he said. Then he paused a moment, thinking. "And you shouldn't be doing physical labor, either, little missy, in case..."

"I'm not pregnant, Dad," said Anne, annoyed now herself. "We've worn out four thermometers over the last six months tracking when I'm ovulating, all for nothing."

Nick winced at too much personal information from a daughter. "Ovulating? Thermometers? Whatever happened to the old fashioned way of making babies?"

Anne sighed. "I wish I knew. We'll ask Gabe when he comes up. He and Manuel are taking another break, their fourth since we started work two hours ago."

Anne, Nick, and Sallie watched Gabe and Manuel as they chatted near the dock. Gabe took off his work gloves and patted Manuel's shoulder. Manuel nodded. Then he ambled off down the incline alone, while Gabe strode in the opposite direction toward the terrace. Halfway up the slope, he called out to his father-in-law. "Hey, man. How're you feeling? Glad to see you outside...fresh air."

Nick held up his tea glass to acknowledge Gabe. "Counting it all for horse manure."

Sallie gave Nick a dirty look, which he returned. He then amended his phrase to Gabe, "Joyful horse manure."

"Speaking of joyful," Gabe said when he stepped onto the terrace. "Manuel just told me that today is his birthday." He leaned over and kissed Anne on her forehead. "You up for a mariachi party tonight, my little Carlita? Dobro guitars? Manuel's famous street corn, salsa, maracas?"

Gabe shook imaginary maracas in the air and rolled his shoulders in a salsa beat. With a smile that required no words, Anne accepted her husband's invitation.

⚝

An open pregnancy test kit lay on the counter in Anne and Gabe's designer bathroom. Anne stood before the vanity mirror, her face set in grim determination. She flinched as she read the results on the meter. Negative...again. Grimacing, she flung the meter into the trash basket. Hands trembling, heart pounding, she gathered up the other parts and pieces of the kit and chucked them into the same basket. Her emotions were surging so high that she had to grip the edge of the counter to keep from screaming. After a few shudders, coughs, and sharp sniffs, she regained her usual stoic control and walked out of the bathroom, though she could not resist slamming the door extra hard.

⚝

Anne sat in the passenger seat of Gabe's truck. He scowled at the road ahead and pressed harder on the accelerator. "I wish I hadn't told you," he said.

Anne braced against the dashboard. Sharp curves on the secondary road did not lend themselves to interstate speeds.

"Did you think I wouldn't have noticed?" she said. "Why are you driving so fast? You're scaring me."

"I'm not driving fast. This right here is driving fast." He sped up another ten miles an hour. "You make me so mad," he said, "pretending you don't get the fact that when Manuel told me his little sister was pregnant, with no husband, no job, and no education...it was man talk, sharing our troubles. Poor guy can't keep up with his bills as it is, and now another mouth to feed."

"Precisely why she ought to give the baby to a responsible couple like us...let us adopt, if it's a boy."

"You'd take her baby if it were a boy, but not a girl? What a lousy attitude. I wish I hadn't told you."

"Why is it God lets girls like Manuel's sister get pregnant and denies great people like us?"

Gabe snorted anger. "I'll let you know when we get great, which will be never."

❦

Manuel and his brothers danced with their wives to the shifting rhythms of an outdoor mariachi band. The dance floor was a series of wide planks laid side by side on the grassy lot next to Manuel's mobile home. It was wobbly, but good enough for fun.

Gabe and Anne entered the party scene late. Finding a parking spot for their crew cab had not been easy. Gabe waved to Manuel, who stopped dancing and dragged his shy wife by her hand over to welcome Anne and Gabe. Manuel grinned and shook Gabe's hand. He seemed genuinely touched when Anne handed him the gift-wrapped birthday present she had brought along. Smiling like a child, he shook the box and spoke in excited Spanish to his wife, to whom he introduced Anne and Gabe with great flourish. The pretty senora nodded and tried to make up for being unable to speak English by leading her new guests to the refreshment table, where Manuel's pregnant sister, Maria, was serving Mexican treats. Gabe's smile curdled when he caught Anne staring at Maria's abdomen, though his irritation was lost on Manuel, who lived his own life laughing out loud at his own capricious circumstances. Satisfied that Gabe and Anne would be happy eating and drinking for a few minutes, Manuel put an arm around his wife's waist and two-stepped her back to the dance floor.

Maria offered Anne and Gabe street corn from a platter. Anne studied Maria; Gabe studied Anne. Just as he was about to tell her that he thought they should be leaving, Manuel's younger brother, Juan, appeared and somehow managed to get Anne on the dance floor. Gabe watched as she tried to keep up with Juan's expert salsa. Juan feigned disappointment when Anne gestured that she was dying of thirst and pulled away.

Gabe, already out of sorts over Anne's unhealthy interest in Maria's baby, became furious when he realized she was now dodging him at every turn. Disgusted, he sat down on a stack of orange crates to bide his time. He watched with nervous eyes as she made her way back to the refreshment table. The mariachi band began a slow dance as she poured herself a cup of lemonade and began zigzagging back through the crowd. A few tired guests departed when the music went soft, but not Anne. She snagged Manuel again and engaged him in conversation. From across the lot, Gabe observed Manuel's expression go from lighthearted to serious as Anne spoke. After a moment, Manuel pointed toward the refreshment table and again led Anne over to Maria. Even from afar, Gabe could tell that Manuel was wasting no time explaining Anne's proposal to his sister, who at first listened intently, then looked frightened. She clutched her belly and ran away into the night, leaving Anne and Manuel with nothing more to discuss.

Gabe got up from the stack of crates and pushed his way across the dance floor. He grabbed Anne's hand and dragged her toward the parking area without saying goodbye to Manuel or anyone else.

Anne tried to extricate herself from her angry husband's grasp. "Stop manhandling me," she said. "You're acting crazy!"

Gabe opened the passenger door to the truck, forced Anne onto the seat, and addressed her through clenched teeth. "Who do you think you are? No one walks up to a little girl like that and asks for her baby. It's criminal."

Anne rubbed her wrist and glared at him. "Manuel didn't think so. He thought it was a great idea for his sister to have a little cash thrown her way for once in her pitiful life."

"Manuel was wrong. You scared her half to death. I didn't realize you were that...desperate."

"Desperate!" Anne shouted. "You don't know what desperate is, what it feels like...not being able to get pregnant month after month. It's not happening to you."

"Oh, it's happening to me all right. I've got a front row

seat to the great Anne York not getting her way for once in her life. You don't care about anybody but yourself. Not that poor girl, me, your sisters, nobody. You want what you want when you want it, like always."

Anne's hysteria changed to a strange calm. "You can't shame me," she said. "It isn't wrong for a woman to want a baby, a son."

"At what cost, whose expense? Don't ever do anything like that again, not while I'm around."

Anne glared in silence at Gabe's flushed face.

ᕬᕬᕬ

Gabe sat on a wooden stool in his garage workshop. Though it was not a real workshop, just a quiet corner beyond the open area where he parked his pickup. Gabe had turned the small space into a respectable mini art studio with a worktable and wall shelves to display his model ships and wooden hand-carvings. A glance at the six shelves, each laden with models, carved doves, angels, crosses, praying hands, and wood-burned *Bible* verse plaques, made it apparent Gabe had spent many long hours assembling, carving, wood-burning, sanding, and polishing.

The self-styled artist hummed along to a praise song on the radio as he worked on the most elaborate project he had ever tackled, a model of the USS *Constitution*, with three masts, twenty-three canvas sails, and four pairs of iron davits. His relaxed demeanor suggested Gabe was a happy man in the presence of his artwork. But the instant he heard Anne's footsteps on the other side of the mudroom door, his mood changed, and not in a good way.

"What now?" he whispered aloud to himself as he replaced the cap on a tube of glue. He did not have to wait long for an answer. The mudroom door flew open, and Anne burst through. Gabe stood motionless as the storm trooper in his life stomped down the short flight of steps to the garage level, leather purse strap slung over her shoulder. Every cell in Gabe's body went on alert. Where could storm trooper be going in such an agitated state? He watched her kick his athletic shoes off the bottom step. Then she leaned down and picked up a furled umbrella that had the misfortune to be in her path and lobbed it over the hood of the truck. Gabe ducked. Two wooden lovebirds and a carving of praying hands hit the floor.

"Watch it," he said, retrieving his sculpted pieces. "Guess this means you're still mad about what went down at Manuel's party. I think I liked the cold shoulder better."

Anne exhaled defeat and leaned against the stair rail. "I'm sorry. I'm not mad, not at you, anyway...just frustrated. Those blockheads at the fertility clinic don't know what they're doing. Six months and eight thousand dollars for what? Nothing happened again this month."

She pressed the button to the automatic garage doors and duck-walked underneath as they went up. Gabe suppressed a chuckle and followed her to the driveway, where he did not make the mistake of trying to help her into the Jaguar. He did, however, express an opinion on her travel plans. "I don't think you ought to go over to the clinic upset like this. You might cause some kind of estrogen bomb to go off...blow up a city block."

"Yeah, the clinic is a waste of time. I'm going to see

Charlotte."

Gabe did not look relieved. "Charlotte?" he said with suspicion. "Okay, a little twosome estrogen tea party could be just as dangerous."

Anne gripped the door handle of the car, but she did not open it. She stiffened her back and closed her eyes. Gabe could tell even from her profile how drawn with fatigue her face had become. After the briefest moment of regrouping, she turned sharply and met his gaze, her green eyes brimming with tears. "I'm running out of time," she said. "Daddy's oncologist told Mom this morning he needs more treatments. His condition...it's getting worse."

Gabe had no response to news that bad. The two of them stood silent for a second, staring into each other's eyes. It was Anne who broke the connection, as if the pain of interacting emotionally with her husband was too much to bear. She climbed into the Jag without speaking and screeched out of the driveway. Gabe stood helpless in the opening to the garage door as she sped away. Squinting in frustration, he muttered under his breath, "Nick isn't the only one getting worse."

— Anne —

Slipping fast is how I had begun to view my diminishing ability to cope with life's challenges. Quite the departure from *skipping fast*, the approach to life for which I had always been known. I am trying hard to be honest in giving you an accurate reading on my "colorful" personality, colorful, that is, before it took such a beating from the monster known as infertility. I admit that my reactions to not being able to get pregnant were no more emotionally charged than those of other women facing the same awful issue. Infertility can make even a placid woman go from upset to neurotic to banging like a maniac on the door of the nearest psychiatric hospital...all in a matter of months. And if you think I'm exaggerating, just suit up in protective gear and ask any woman who has experienced infertility to tell you her story. Don't get me wrong. I'm not making excuses for my behavior, or the behavior of any other woman. What I am saying is this...I'm not the only one who has lost her footing in the desert of childlessness. And yet, looking back, I realize suffering through it taught me many important lessons - profound lessons - that I may never have learned any other way, one of which was the folly of thinking I could control my life through personal will alone.

Any woman who has spent years believing a prideful thing like that, and then crashes into a brick wall like infertility, is bound to collapse emotionally in an exceedingly short amount of time, as short as half a year in my case. But the current question is...why am I sharing this information with you? And the current answer is...I eventually became thankful for being brought so low. How else would I have learned that my human weakness is God's strength, or found my way back into his fold again, or learned humility, sympathy, gratitude, even love. Your own trial may be something other than infertility. My dad would say his was cancer. But every one of us, at some time or another, will encounter a difficulty that seems insurmountable. My hope is you will not react to yours in the same self-destructive way that I did. It took someone intensely arrogant (me!) to forget, or just plain ignore, God's immutable sovereignty and goodness in all situations, including my battle, indeed, my war with infertility. No wonder I was Spiritually deaf to his wisdom for such a long, dry time. Thank you, God, for never ceasing to call out to me. I am grateful you gave me Spiritual ears to hear you, along with a heart to answer your call. Great is your faithfulness, Lord Jesus! Great is your faithfulness! Amen.

Before his downfall a man's heart is proud,
but humility comes before honor.
PROVERBS 18:12 CSB

(from Mary's Song – the Magnificat)
He (God) has performed mighty deeds with his arm;
he has scattered those who are proud
in their inmost thoughts.
He has brought down rulers from their thrones
but has lifted up the humble.
LUKE 1:51-52 NIV

For I can do everything through Christ,
who gives me strength.
PHILIPPIANS 4:13 NLT

God is my strength and power:
and he maketh my way perfect.
2 SAMUEL 22:33 KJV

Seek the Lord and his strength;
seek his presence continually!
1 CHRONICLES 16:11 ESV

In quietness and in trust is your strength.
ISAIAH 30:15B NIV

Trust in the Lord with all your heart and lean not on your
own understanding; in all your ways submit to him,
and he will make your paths straight.
PROVERBS 3:5-6 NIV

Don't be afraid, for I am with you. Don't be discouraged,
for I am your God. I will strengthen you and help you.
I will hold you up with my victorious right hand.
ISAIAH 41:10 NLT

[Paul] But he (God) said to me, "My grace is sufficient
for you, for my power is made perfect in weakness."
2 CORINTHIANS 12:9A ESV

Chapter

Anne's middle sister, Charlotte, concentrated on scraping blue paint off an antique chair leg. Dried paint of many more colors streaked her faded overalls, attesting to her long interest in refinishing furniture under the shade of the massive pecan tree in her backyard. Little Annie, Charlotte's three-year-old, played alone in her sandbox nearby. As Little Annie dug in the sand, a figure approaching from the side yard next to the house caught her mother's protective eye. She smiled on realizing it was not an intruder, but her sister.

"Hey," Charlotte yelled to Anne. Then she turned to her little one and said, "Look who's here, baby girl. It's your name sake."

Anne barely acknowledged Charlotte before calling out in loving tones to Little Annie. "Hi there, sweet doll. I brought you something."

She held up a pack of gum. Little Annie grinned and ran toward her. Anne bent down and hugged her laughing niece. Little Annie clapped her hands for the gum. Anne gave it to her, whispering, "Don't tell Mama. She might say no."

She helped Little Annie unwrap the gum and get a piece into her mouth. Then she took her niece's hand and walked her back to the sandbox where she joined her in filling a bucket with sand.

Charlotte cocked her head at Anne. "Something's going on," she said. "And you came to tell it. Are you...?"

Anne wiped her hands on her slacks and took a seat in a lawn chair next to the sandbox. "Not even close. Months of pills, injections, treatments, money, money, money. And for what...a big fat zero."

"Oh, honey," Charlotte said. "Don't give up. Everyone knows it takes more time for some of us. My friend, Ellie Pardue, spent a year at that same clinic before she got pregnant. She was a wreck over it...acted just like Hannah in the Bible...crying all the time, begging God in prayer."

"I don't know Ellie Pardue, and I don't know Hannah in the *Bible*. Neurotic women make me sick." Anne then examined her pinkie fingernail and bit it...neurotically.

Charlotte leaned forward and laughed at her. "You don't know Ellie, 'cause she lives downtown on Monterey Square in Savannah's high rent district. And Hannah's been living in the *Old Testament* for centuries in *First Samuel*, Chapter One. Poor thing got so emotionally overwrought about not being able to get pregnant that she cried herself sick praying in the temple...literally flung herself on the floor and made a vow before God, which everybody knows you aren't supposed to do. And when Eli, the priest, saw her bawling and carrying on, he thought she'd been drinking. Gave her a piece of his mind for coming in the temple and acting out like that. But when she told him she wasn't drunk, that she just wanted a baby really badly, he dropped all his priestly duties and started praying for her then and there, and lo and behold, God gave her a son...in the fullness of time, of course. She named him

Samuel, 'cause she asked the Lord for him. Must be what the name, Samuel, means. I don't know about that part."

Charlotte paused and took a quick breath. Anne's eyes had practically spiraled at the details of her sister's story, most of which she found ridiculous.

Charlotte furrowed her pretty brow and added for current interest, "I don't know if Ellie Pardue threw a crying fit in the church in front of her own preacher. Wouldn't be surprised, though."

Anne interrupted her sister's patter with a bombshell. "Will you be a surrogate for me, Charlotte? Carry a baby for Gabe and me?"

Charlotte went rigid, speechless. She dropped her brush and turned over an open can of paint thinner. Anne grew impatient watching her sister fumble with trying to right the can.

"Well?" she said to the flustered Charlotte.

Who spluttered back, "I don't have but one kidney...with stage two damage after Little Annie was born. Every doctor I've ever seen has told me not to get pregnant again. And Thomas is still off in his bachelor pad trying to find himself. I have no help with Little Annie, and now Mom needs me to do shifts tending to Daddy."

Charlotte, now rattled to the core, stopped speaking and held her breath, as if searching her brain for some way Anne's idea might work. After a moment, she gave up and admitted defeat. "I don't think my body could take it."

Anne looked disgusted. She leaned forward in the lawn chair and said with a tone approaching anger, "Your body would be fine. I'm a gynecologist. I've seen lots of women with one kidney have healthy babies and get along great."

"But I didn't have a healthy baby. Little Annie…"

"Your kidney problems had nothing to do with her presenting with Down's. That's a chromosome thing." Now it was Anne's turn to pause. She fixed Charlotte with a burning stare and asked again, "Will you?"

"But the doctors say I could die. How could I risk that with Little Annie depending on me? She can't count on Thomas for anything. He's too freaked out about her Down's."

Charlotte began weeping. Anne stood up and brushed sand from her clothing. "I understand," she said. "It's all right. I see."

She turned from Charlotte and started walking toward the back corner of the house, the direction from which she had come. Charlotte, weeping openly now, called after her. "Wait, Anne, please. I've got Little Annie to take care of. Stop…"

"So take care of her," Anne said, her voice trembling. "I'll figure out another way."

Anne flicked away her own tears and stepped up her pace. Charlotte slumped into the nearest lawn chair and gave in to sobbing the instant Anne disappeared around the house. Little Annie stumbled over and buried her face in her mother's lap, weeping because her mother was weeping.

✺

Rose and Charlotte sat with their mother, Sallie, at the York kitchen table the morning after Anne's terrible request.

Charlotte choked her way through an explanation of the backyard scene with Anne. Sallie went white with shock. Rose turned crimson with fury. Scraping her chair legs on the tile floor, she stood and headed toward the dining room archway that opened to the living area.

Sallie called to her. "Rose...where are you going?"

But Rose did not look back. She walked faster as she responded to her mother with a knife-edged tone. "To tell Daddy what Anne has done to Charlotte."

Sallie bolted out of her chair and chased after her oldest daughter. "No, you can't. He's already having a bad day." She caught her daughter's arm and held her back.

Rose stopped and twisted out of Sallie's grasp. "He needs to know, Mom...how she's hurting our family. Charlotte is crushed. Daddy has to open his eyes, see the truth."

"It's too late," Sallie said. "He's sick. Isn't it enough Charlotte's torn up?"

Rose's lips quivered. "Charlotte isn't the only one."

"You're right," Sallie said, trembling. "We all are. But can't you see? Anne's pain is the worst. She doesn't even have proper faith to help her through. Put yourself in her shoes. How would you feel if...?"

"You're not being fair, Mom. Not to Charlotte, me, not even yourself. You never have been. Daddy hasn't, either. I know God commands us to forgive, but it's hard when a person never changes. What are we supposed to do? Forgive her for the same old kinds of selfish behaviors 'til we all drop dead? I, for one, am done. You don't have to worry, though. I won't tell Daddy. What good would it do? He'd defend her, which I could not stomach."

Rose switched the direction of her path so abruptly that she almost made her mother fall. Not even noticing, Rose continued her tirade as she strode toward her new destination, the front door. "But you can't stop me from calling Gabe," she said. "Somebody has to tell him what his wife is up to."

Sallie stood silent after Rose disappeared in a whoosh through the doorway to the front piazza. She had wanted to say more to her upset daughter, but it was useless to speak again after the door clicked shut. She leaned against the wall of her spacious hallway, looking older than her years...old and tired and defeated.

— *Anne* —

Can you believe I thought the ache of my infertility was about no one else beyond myself? I was able to see to a small degree it was also about Gabe, but my focus remained *me, me, me... self, self, self*. I did not know, nor did I care, how badly my increasing emotional instability was hurting those around me. I couldn't see that my disintegration was a consequence of building my life upon the shifting sands of personal strength (or lack thereof) instead of God, the Rock. And yet, despite my foolishness, God never stopped loving me and reaching out, no matter how unlovable I became. And trust me, injuring others was the mere surface evidence of my decline. Day by day, I found myself sinking deeper into a dark pit of my own making. By choice, will, and habit, I made my default mode looking downward into that shadowy abyss rather than upward toward Jesus. Such was the condition of my soul. The amazing thing was even in my unworthiness, Jesus still cared for me with the same agape love with which he cares for all his children. Thank you, Lord, for your gifts of grace and faith and for the joy and peace with which I finally accepted your mercy. Amen.

> [Jesus] *Therefore everyone who hears these words of mine and puts them into practice is like a wise man who built his house on the rock. The rain came down, the streams rose, and the winds blew and beat against that house; yet it did not fall, because it had its foundation on the rock. But everyone who hears these words of mine and does not put them into practice is like a foolish man who built his house on sand. The rain came down, the streams rose, and the winds blew and beat against that house,*

and it fell with a great crash.
MATTHEW 7:24-27 NIV

But God demonstrates his own love for us in this:
While we were still sinners, Christ died for us.
ROMANS 5:8 NIV

Chapter

Dr. Mark Armond rested his elbows on his desk and stared at Anne. He had guessed in his first appointment with the Yorks as a couple that she was the more volatile of the two, though he did not realize the advanced extent. He phrased his response with care. "We usually wait a little longer before moving on to more involved procedures like in vitro fertilization, Mrs. York...Dr. York. You've only been with us six months."

Anne returned Dr. Armond's professional gaze without blinking. As much a degreed physician as he, she had no intention of being intimidated by his superior attitude. "My father is terminally ill," she said to the male ego across the desk. "I want him to see his first grandson before he dies."

"No father would put that kind of pressure on a daughter," said the ego. "You're doing this to yourself...and to your husband, I'm guessing, since he didn't come with you today." Dr. Armond waited a second before continuing. His patient's stubborn attitude told him he was going to have no luck convincing her of anything against her will, certainly not the imprudence of rushing into IVF. Said he with no hope of being agreed with by a woman as proud as the one sitting before him, "Although recent research studies do not support it, I still go along with the idea that stress can be a factor in infertility. And, frankly, you seem highly stressed. Have you considered counseling? Many women in your position have benefited from..."

Anne cut him off mid-phrase. "I want to move forward with in vitro as quickly as possible," she said. "Will you help or not?"

"Can you and your husband afford the fees? It's expensive and with no promise of a child, which makes it doubly nerve wracking."

"We'll find the money. I'll find it by myself if I have to."

"All right, but you must understand from the outset, IVF does *not* provide guaranteed success. Less than five percent of couples who have trouble conceiving ever go as far as IVF. And within that small group, in your age range, only forty-five percent or so end up with a baby."

"I know the stats. I'm a GYN. What do we do first to get started?"

"First? First you write a sizable check."

Anne flinched and tried to cover it, but Dr. Armond's sharp eyes saw. He leaned forward and opened a small, hinged box on his desk, took out a business card, and pushed it across the desk toward Anne. She picked it up and read the fancy script aloud: *"Confidential Infertility Support Groups - Lucinda Maybank, Psychologist."*

Dr. Armond made eye contact with Anne before speaking again. "I never recommend anyone else. Lucinda Maybank has been running infertility groups for years, long before I opened this clinic. Can't hurt. Might help."

Anne laid the card face down on Dr. Armond's desk and

stood up with a false show of confidence. "Now that you and I are on the same page, I won't be needing a psychologist."

She turned and walked toward the door, but stopped on reaching it, one hand motionless on the doorknob. Dr. Armond gave her a moment of silence, after which she came back to his desk, retrieved the card, and met his gaze with a slightly softer expression. "Maybe you're right," she said. "Meeting a few other women going through the same thing might be a good idea. Who knows? Maybe I could be of help to one or two."

Dr. Armond chuckled in spite of himself.

❦

At Anne's insistence that she and Gabe deserved special attention for the evening, the maître d' of *Savor Savannah Restaurant* guided the two of them toward the best table in the house. Anne's eyes sparkled at Gabe across the table after they were seated. Her beautiful face glowed in the candlelight as she relayed to her apprehensive husband details of her latest appointment with Dr. Armond.

Anyone in hearing distance would have picked up on the fact that Anne's speech was too fast for normal. Was she afraid Gabe was going to interrupt? Disagree? Pose some reasonable question from the dreaded realm of common sense? Anne seemed determined to leave no room in the air space for any contradictory word from Gabe. Her words flew at him rapid-fire over the table's tea rose centerpiece. "...and because I'm still in the youngest age range, I've got close to a fifty percent chance for success. In vitro fertilization, IVF...it's commonplace now. Everybody's doing it."

She glanced around the upscale restaurant, the owners of which had spared no expense in creating the illusion of romantic ambience. "This is my kind of place," she said to her mute husband. "It's perfect for taking control of our lives...finally!"

Gabe had not eaten a bite. He could not. The more Anne talked, the more the knot in his stomach tightened. "Everybody is doing it?" he said.

A look of irritation passed over Anne's face, but she dismissed it in favor of her new positive attitude. In jerky phrases that lurched along in overtime, she began making her case again. "Yes, Gabe. Everybody who is serious about dealing with infertility, like me, like us. IVF is not as complicated as people think. They'll get me all prepped with injections and instructions, harvest some of my eggs when it's time, and then fertilize them in a lab situation in a petri dish, using your collected sperm. *In vitro* literally means in glass. And in five or six days, after the fertilized eggs have developed into viable embryos, Dr. Armond will help us decide how many we need to transfer to my uterus and how many to freeze. You can even select your baby's gender if you want. Isn't that an amazing option? You know I want a boy for Daddy's sake."

"Gender selection...seems kind of...I don't know...extreme. I'm afraid to ask how they do a thing like that. And what does freeze mean? I don't like the sound of it."

"They freeze the leftover embryos to save for later..." Anne's voice had picked up a measure of strain that she hoped Gabe would not detect. "...in case I don't get pregnant the first or second time around. It's called cryopreservation.

84

And everybody really is doing it."

"But what if you do get pregnant? What happens to the little leftovers?"

"We give our permission to discard them."

"Discard?"

"Or save them for later, down the road."

Gabe drew his brows together involuntarily. "But down the road...after we have all the children we can afford, and we still have some leftovers in the freezer at the clinic...what then?"

"We discard them...then...or donate them for stem cell research."

Gabe sat far back in his chair, almost as if he were disengaging himself from the entire meal, the entire room, the entire discussion. "No, no. I couldn't do that. I couldn't. No."

Anne's optimism disappeared in a whoosh. Her face paled under her makeup. "Gabe," she rasped, "you can't put me through one egg at a time retrieval, at fifteen thousand dollars a clip, and risk failure of implanting a single embryo that might not even be viable? That's insane."

Gabe removed his napkin from his lap and placed it in a wad by his plate. "I don't see how we can do it any other way, if by retrieval you mean taking an egg from your ovary."

"No one in their right mind retrieves a single egg, Gabe... not on purpose. Lead-up meds to prepare the ovaries are difficult physically, not to mention the emotional roller coaster they cause hormonally. It would be senseless to try IVF with the plan of retrieving one egg."

"Senseless or not, I can't be a part of it any other way."

"But no clinic will agree to that. You need to retrieve several eggs, as many viable ones as you can get to make sure you have enough backups when some of them fail. And even then, they could all fail, and you'd have to make the decision about whether to go through a whole new cycle of IVF for more tries, which is more money. I don't think you'd ever be able to find a clinic that would go along with intentionally retrieving one egg."

"I'm sorry," Gabe said. "I didn't understand how complicated this could get. But for me to go along with giving it a try, we can do one egg retrieval at a time, so there won't be any leftovers after fertilization. Which means one embryo at a time. That's it. For this family, there will be no discarding of embryos fertilized for backups."

Anne put a hand to her temple and stared hard at Gabe. "Why are you being so dogmatic about this?" she said through clenched teeth. "Don't you know how upsetting it is for me?"

"Me, too," Gabe said. "This is the first time since we've been married I've had to say a flat no to you, except for that sorry business with Manuel's sister. Right now, I'm thinking I should've said no to a lot of other unreasonableness... huge car payments, massive mortgage, fancy vacations we couldn't afford. But with this, I don't have a choice. I'm saying no, like your sister had to say no to being a surrogate. Rose called and told me about that. She said you broke Charlotte's heart. What's the matter with you? The girl has one kidney, and it weak."

Anne got up from the table and held onto its edge. An observer would have guessed she'd had too much to drink, which was not the case. Her napkin slid to the floor. Shallow of breath, red of face, she explained in a voice breaking on every other syllable exactly what had gotten into her. "Rose and Charlotte don't understand anything about what I'm going through," she said. "And apparently, you don't, either. I didn't mean to hurt Charlotte. I was trying to find some practical way to have a child."

Choking on a sob, she wheeled around and rushed toward the restaurant door, not quite getting there before tears came. Gabe, near tears himself, stood and watched her go, making no move to try to stop her.

— *Anne* —

I was too keyed up to sleep after I got home from our disastrous evening at *Savor Savannah*. I had taken the Jag and left Gabe stranded. Who knew how he was going to get home, or when, or if? I did not care. I camped out in the guest room for the rest of the night, worrying, fretting, trying to think how to make my blockhead husband see the positive aspects of ART – Assisted Reproductive Technology. I told myself he would come around after he got over being squeamish. Though even I, a medical doctor with a high regard for science, had already found it necessary to harden myself to the idea that all medical options associated with ART, including questionable ones, were acceptable in civilized society these days. I had convinced myself they were simply distasteful means to a positive end, Gabe's shocked reaction notwithstanding. My hard and fast opinion at the time was simple...when infertility was an issue for a couple, the husband had an obligation to help his wife bear a child any way he could, to include putting aside his Christian convictions.

> [Paul] *For I know that nothing good dwells in me, that is, in my flesh. For I have the desire to do what is right, but not the ability to carry it out. For I do not do the good I want, but the evil I do not want is what I keep on doing. Now if I do what I do not want, it is no longer I doing it, but sin that dwells within me. Wretched man that I am! Who will deliver me from this body of death? Thanks be to God through Jesus Christ our Lord!*
> **ROMANS 7:18-20; 24-25A ESV**

Chapter

10

Again, Gabe found himself seeking solace in his workshop, the one peaceful corner of the house. But this time he focused on his smart tablet screen rather than paint and glue. "Cryopreservation, freezing embryos," he read aloud. "Discarding, destroying extra embryos. Selective reduction, terminating embryos inside the womb when too many have successfully implanted. Possible reason for selective reduction...too many embryos that implant successfully may result in compromising the health of the mother and wanted embryos. Insert needle and inject selected embryos to be terminated with potassium chloride."

Gabe gasped and looked away from the tablet. He squeezed his eyes shut and covered his mouth and chin with his free hand. "*Dear God,*" he breathed.

Anne entered Gabe's workshop area without his hearing her. He startled when her footsteps penetrated his whirling thoughts. With a quick flip of the tablet screen cover, he hid what he had been reading. His face remained gray and tense.

Anne took a seat on the stool next to Gabe's and spoke first, her voice thin with raw nerves. Lack of sleep had drained all color from her usual peaches and cream complexion. "Hello," she said. "I came out here to tell you

I'm sorry for losing my temper. You know, at the restaurant. I'm not mad at you or anyone else...not at Rose, Charlotte, no one. I'm...on edge all the time, like I might jump out of my own skin. The clinic nurses warned me some women get like this. Those hormone injections I've been taking are brutal, throw you into crazy land. Anyway, I apologize if I came across as unfeeling about some of the procedures that go with IVF. I forget I'm a medical person and you're not."

She waited for a response, but Gabe said nothing, just kept his eyes fixed on the model ship dominating his worktable. His silence confused Anne. It was not Gabe's usual style to create distance between them, much less harbor it in such an obvious manner.

"Wow," she said. "From the look on your face, I definitely should have waited a little longer to try to explain IVF...or maybe let Dr. Armond do it. He's better at softening the unpleasant aspects. Anyway, I'll call the clinic first thing tomorrow and make another appointment. We can go in together...if you're willing."

Gabe, still unable to connect with Anne, looked as if he might break down and cry. She touched his forearm. "Are you all right, Gabe? Surely you don't mind talking things over with Dr. Armond, discuss costs, if nothing else. No one can afford to do IVF with the limits you were talking about. We're already over what we budgeted even for the less complicated procedures. Are you still mad at me? If you are, what about Manuel's sister? Maybe she changed her mind after the baby was born. Maybe it's too hard for her, being a single mom."

Gabe emerged from his trance, though the effort appeared difficult. "Uh, no, no," he said. I'm not mad...worried...all the stuff that's gotten out of control in our lives. And not only IVF. I haven't been able to work up the courage to tell you, but, well...I got laid off Friday, out of nowhere, indefinitely. Jet Air lost some big contracts. They're having to shut down a whole division."

Anne's body went rigid. She jerked her hand off Gabe's arm and put it to her throat. "You mean...no more paychecks?"

Gabe made eye contact with his shocked wife, though it was apparent he would rather have slunk away to some dark hiding place. "Don't freak," he said. "I'll start looking for something else tomorrow."

"But we're barely scraping by as it is, and now we need more money for the clinic. I can't depend on you for anything."

Gabe lost his composure under the sting of Anne's insult. His hurt came blustering out in a harsh tone. "I told you. I'll find something. We have to keep up the payments on our million-dollar mortgage for this monster mansion you had to have to impress everybody. Who does that...goes in debt a million bucks for a stupid house?"

Anne clenched her teeth. "Doctors do that," she said, "because they can. I'm not taking the blame for you losing your job. All I want is a baby, and you can't even give me that."

"A baby is flavor of the month. You live your life in a constant state of want...want this, want that, want a bunch of junk better than everybody else's junk. This house, that Jag you drive around in like you think you're some kind of celeb."

He shoved the tablet to the back of the table and stood up, so angry that his hands were trembling. "I thought you'd settle down after a while, get satisfied. But you ain't gonna. I should have known."

Anne stood also and glared at Gabe. "I don't have to take this kind of abuse," she said. "Get out."

He balled up his fists and stepped into her personal space. "Did you forget my name is on the mortgage, too?" he said. "And the vehicle loans and two personal loans? No way you can keep those payments afloat without my hefty, yet always belittled paychecks. And what about IVF? How're you going to pull that one off without me?"

"I don't need you. I'll use a sperm donor if I have to. There's always a way at the clinic. All it takes is money. Now get out!"

"Yeah, I hear money can buy anything these days. Go ahead, run to Daddy Nick for the dough. But you'd better not tell him every little detail about what you're planning to do. That would be cruel. He's too weak to bear up."

"I'll do whatever I want. He's my father, not yours."

"True, unfortunately. By the way, I've been doing some reading on my tablet here about Assisted Reproductive Technology. Found a bunch of misleading words for harsh procedures. Freezing, discarding, selective reduction. Yeah, selective reduction. That's the worst, killing unwanted embryos inside the womb if too many implant successfully and put the mother and wanted embryo at risk. You expect me to be okay with that, too?"

Anne's face flushed, then drained to white. "Get your stuff and leave. I'm through talking."

Gabe kept on with his rant as if Anne had not spoken. "Let's say they insert four embryos into your uterus from in vitro, hoping at least one will implant, but then all of them implant unexpectedly. That'll be okay, though, 'cause you can use selective reduction to kill off the three you don't want by injecting them with potassium chloride." He stopped talking, leaving an acrid pause in the air before shouting as loud as he could, *"I can't do that! I won't!"*

Anne, sobbing now, rushed from the workshop space, toppling a wooden stool in the process. Gabe scowled at the partially completed model of the tall ship on his worktable, then he cleared the surface with a forearm, barely missing his tablet. The delicate model shattered into jagged fragments on the concrete floor.

⟨⟨⟨⟨

Roadside Dream Motel's vacancy light above the entrance blinked a blue invitation to weary travelers, Gabe's unintended status after his fight with Anne. He turned over in bed and looked around at the depressing room, then face planted back into the pillow.

Home alone, Anne awoke in her and Gabe's bedroom. She groaned and opened her eyes, realizing no more sleep was to be had. Swinging her feet to the side of the bed and sitting up, she took her purse from the night table. Rummaging through it, she found Lucinda Maybank's business card that Dr. Armond had given her. After a second of staring at the tasteful script and feminine graphic on the crumpled card, she picked up her smart phone and keyed in Maybank's number.

— *Anne* —

Satan, the original liar, is skilled at luring us down wrong roads. I should have been praying and asking Jesus, the Good Shepherd, for guidance, but instead, I sought counsel from Lucinda Maybank, a total stranger. I was afraid if I asked God what to do, he would close the door on some of the medical options offered by the fertility clinic, options I had persuaded myself might be of help. I figured a modern woman with a business card flaunting a PhD after her name would be less rigid than God in what she thought would be okay. For I was not seeking Spiritual wisdom to inform my decisions. I was seeking worldly permission to do whatever was expedient to get my way and feel good about it in the company of other women who had adopted the same mindset. Tolerant women. Modern, strong, open-minded women. Surely a group led by a professional in the field of psychology would be able to come up with a few reasonable suggestions about how an infertile woman with no support from her closest family members should proceed. Surely.

Thus says the Lord: "Cursed is the man who trusts in man and makes flesh his strength, whose heart turns away from the Lord. He is like a shrub in the desert and shall not see any good come. He shall dwell in the parched places of the wilderness, in an uninhabited salt land. Blessed is the man who trusts in the Lord, whose trust is the Lord. He is like a tree planted by water, that sends out its roots by the stream, and does not fear when heat comes, for its leaves remain green, and it is not anxious in the year of drought, for it does not cease to bear fruit."

JEREMIAH 17:5-8 ESV

Chapter

11

Charlotte pushed Little Annie on a swing at Marsh Bank Park, a popular playground in their neighborhood that boasted every kind of outdoor play system known to childhood. Other parents helicoptered around their offspring as some of the more adventuresome tykes risked life and limb on the climbing wall and roundabout.

Gabe walked across the grass wearing the same wrinkled clothes he had slept in at Roadside Dream Motel. He stopped long enough to deposit his smart tablet on the picnic table beside Charlotte's boat bag. Then he strode toward the play area for preschoolers where Charlotte and Little Annie had taken up residence.

When Little Annie spied Gabe, she scrambled off the swing and ran to meet him. He caught her up in his arms and swung her around, laughing and teasing. She giggled and begged for more, but Gabe feigned a sore knee, took her by her tiny hand, and led her back toward her mother.

Charlotte smiled and called out to Gabe. "Hi there. How did you find us?"

"Mama Sallie," he called back. "I had a hankering to see my favorite niece." Still holding Little Annie's hand, he gestured toward the picnic table. All three settled themselves on the sandy benches.

"Give Uncle Gabe a kiss, Annie," Charlotte said to her child.

Little Annie kissed Gabe on his cheek and hugged him again. Charlotte was all smiles over the wonderful outing her little girl was enjoying. "Why don't you go play on the monkey bars, sweetheart," she said. "You're big enough to do that by yourself now."

Little Annie ran to the smallest jungle gym and began climbing and laughing with the other children. Charlotte and Gabe kept watchful eyes on her as they chatted. Charlotte pressed Gabe for the real reason he had come by. "What's going on? Is it Anne?"

"Yeah, I came to tell you how bad I feel...you know, about what she asked you to do. This baby thing has gotten out of hand. I never thought I'd see her lose it like this."

"Is she still upset 'cause I couldn't...?"

"Upset is putting mildly, but not just with you, with everybody, mostly me. Somehow her not being able to get pregnant has gotten around to my fault. And Nick's illness is making things worse. Anne's afraid he's going to die before she has a baby. I think she might be on the edge of a breakdown. Nurses at the fertility clinic say that happens sometimes to women who can't get pregnant. It's no wonder...the stress of it all. I feel like I might break down myself."

Gabe picked up his tablet and touched the screen. He found the reference he was looking for and the correct spot in the text. Handing the tablet to Charlotte, he showed her where to look. "Read that," he said. "It's enough to mess with anybody's mind."

Charlotte began reading aloud. "In vitro fertilization, IVF. I know what that is. A friend of mine in Junior League went through it. Worked, too. They had twins. She talks about IVF all the time now...how great it was for their family."

"Did she mention the fine print? Scroll down." He pointed to a different paragraph.

Charlotte read the new text aloud, as well. "Cryopreservation...freezing sperm, or eggs, or both, even embryos, for later use."

Gabe kept pointing to more locations on the screen as Charlotte scanned the text, reading aloud in fits and starts. Gabe interrupted her. "Look at what they say about discarding and selective reduction."

Charlotte's face went taut as she read. She looked up at Gabe, her eyes round with surprise and confusion. "Anne is okay with all this?" she said.

"She's at the end of her rope...would be okay with anything that got her a baby. You of all people know that. I'm sick about it."

Charlotte read a few more words. "Discarding extra embryos. Destroying..."

"I've already said no to that, which didn't go well on the home front."

Charlotte kept reading in a murmur. "Selective reduction, also known as selective abortion, refers to choosing to abort a fetus, or fetuses, typically in a multi-fetal pregnancy to decrease health risks to the mother in carrying and giving birth to more than one or two babies...decreases the risk of complications to the remaining fetus or fetuses. The term also includes performing the same procedure when a fetus is likely to be born with a birth defect."

Charlotte jerked her head up and locked eyes with Gabe. "Like Little Annie?" she said, "Down Syndrome? And other things?"

"That's what it says."

"Are you saying Anne thought *that* was okay? And my friend, the one with the twins...?"

"Don't judge her or anybody else who's been through IVF. Every case is individual. People choose different stopping points along the way on how far they're willing to go with procedures. You and I can't sit in judgment."

"What about you, Gabe? How far are you willing to go?"

"Well, no selective reduction, no discarding embryos, no gender selection. Sounds easy enough to decide, but it isn't, once you're into it. Like if you find out through genetic screening an embryo is going to have a terrible medical problem, what then? I've been doing a lot of reading. It's not just a little bit confusing. It's off-the-chart confusing."

"What about Anne? Which parts are confusing to her?"

"Stop right there. I'm not going to let anyone attack Anne because of this. She's an emotional mess right now, a situation I made worse last night, getting all self-righteous about the clinic procedures I didn't like. My attitude was so pompous that Anne lost her temper. And she blew up totally when she found out I lost my job last Friday."

"Oh, no. That's awful."

"Great timing, huh."

"But why is it a problem? Doesn't Anne's practice bring in enough money."

"Nowhere near. You wouldn't believe how much we owe on the house alone, plus all our other junk, not to mention the fees at that high-dollar clinic. Did you know IVF costs over $15,000 a clip?"

"So...Anne hasn't been able to get pregnant, and you said no to her about procedures that she's okay with and you're not, and your job went up in smoke...all at the same time. I'm surprised you lived to tell about any of it."

"That ain't all. She threw me out last night. I had to bunk in at a motel. You're looking at a first-class loser, not exactly York family material."

"Anybody can get laid off. You've got to go talk with Pastor Seabrook, clear your head. He was a huge help to me when Little Annie was born with Down's. I thought I was going to lose my mind after Thomas left us high and dry." She squinted toward the street at a car she recognized. "Speaking of whom, look who just drove up."

Gabe followed Charlotte's gaze toward the curb where a Toyota was easing to a stop. Charlotte's husband, Thomas, got out and walked in long strides toward the picnic table. "Hey, Gabe," he said. "How's it going, man?"

Gabe stood and shook Thomas' hand. "Can't complain. Good to see you, Tom. Been a while."

Thomas shrugged and turned his attention toward his sullen wife. "Listen, Charlotte..."

She cut him off mid-sentence. "It's not your day to visit. The judge said..."

"I know what the judge said. I was hoping you'd grown a heart by now. Sallie told me y'all were over here."

Thomas looked beyond Charlotte and Gabe at Little Annie playing on the jungle gym. "Is she old enough to be on that thing by herself?" he said. "Getting so big now."

Charlotte ignored his concern and gave his vehicle at the curb another hard look. "Is that your girlfriend in the car?"

"I don't have a girlfriend. It's my mom. She wants to see Little Annie before heading back to Atlanta later today."

Charlotte blushed, embarrassed to see Thomas' mother instead of the mythical *other woman* getting out of his Toyota. "Oh," she said quickly, "I guess you can take her for an ice cream cone or something and drop her off at Mother's when you're done." She glanced at her watch. "I have to be over there by four to help with Daddy."

"Mom will appreciate that," said Thomas. "Good to see you, Gabe. Say hey to Anne."

Thomas walked toward the spot where Little Annie was playing. He scooped her into his arms as she ran toward him. Charlotte and Gabe watched as he carried his small preschooler to his mother by the Toyota. Little Annie threw her arms around her grandma's neck.

Charlotte's face stiffened as she observed her child's joy and happiness. Her usually sweet voice turned bitter. "You'd better call Pastor Seabrook before I beat you to it," she said to Gabe. "Thomas has turned me into a bigger nut case than you and Anne put together."

"If you say so," Gabe said. "I can't help but feel sorry for Seabrook. If he got rid of all the nut cases in his congregation, he wouldn't have anybody left."

— *Anne* —

Gabe was right when he told Charlotte I was on the edge. He and I both were, though we could not have been more different in how we were handling our problems. I was busy searching out secular people for advice (like Lucinda Maybank), while Gabe sought guidance from fellow Christians (like Charlotte and Pastor Seabrook). Not that his choice made his quest for right any easier. Take Charlotte, for example, his initial confidante. Some of the more radical procedures available to treat infertility offended her so deeply that Gabe ended up having to counsel her to put aside her judgmental attitudes. Didn't she see that judging others was equally as sinful as anything I might be getting up to at the clinic? What an excellent target I had become for goody-goods like Charlotte and Rose, even my parents. Christians may not go completely tone deaf to God's teachings, but they can be plenty hard-of-hearing on some occasions, one of the reasons believers need to keep company with one another. God wants us to join hearts in dealing mercifully with each other's faults as we follow his wisdom in forgiving. That's what Gabe was trying to communicate to Charlotte at the playground when he reminded her that I was drowning and needed to be rescued by compassion and grace, not bludgeoned by judgment and punishment. Our Lord explained the concept best in *Mark 2:17A ESV* "*It is not the healthy who need a doctor, but the sick. I have not come to call the righteous, but sinners.*"

[Jesus] *Let him who is without sin among you*
be the first to throw a stone.
JOHN 8:7B ESV

Chapter

12

Lucinda Maybank occupied the facilitator's position in front of a half-circle of four women seated in folding chairs. A fifth chair sat empty on the left end. Two of the participants chatted together in soft voices as Lucinda finished filling out a form on her clipboard. After scrawling her signature at the bottom of the page, she glanced at the wall clock. "Five after seven," she said in a singsong. "We should get started."

In the background, a faint click signaled that someone had opened the door to the large room. Every woman turned to stare at Anne as she stepped inside. She paused and stared back.

Lucinda put on her phoniest welcome face. "Oh, hi there," she exclaimed. "So glad you decided to come. I wasn't sure you would after our phone conversation. I included a chair for you, though...just in case."

She pointed toward the empty seat. Anne blushed, inhaled, blinked a few times. Then she walked over and sat down. Lucinda smiled at her. "Welcome to the group," she said. "This is Anne, everyone. Anne, meet Nell, Brenda, Renee, and Maureen."

Each woman acknowledged Anne in turn. Renee, the only African American in the group, was also the only one who smiled at Anne. Except for Lucinda, of course, the pretender who Anne sized up as having the capacity to grin her way through a train wreck.

"Okay then," said the leader/pretender with alarming enthusiasm, considering the sad reason for the group's existence. "Who wants to go first tonight?"

✦✦✦

Pastor Seabrook sat at his desk scrutinizing the fidgety Gabe opposite him in the visitor's chair. Gabe could not tolerate a single second of silence in their conversation. His frayed nerves affected even his voice. "Thanks for seeing me so late, Pastor. My problem isn't really an emergency, I guess."

Pastor Seabrook leaned forward and peered at Gabe over the scratched lenses of his pharmacy readers. His countenance was intense. "Oh, it's an emergency all right," he said. "When a woman wants to have a baby and can't, it's volcanic!"

✦✦✦

"About to explode! That's what I feel like," said the well-put-together woman seated next to Anne. Her name was Maureen, or that's the name Anne thought she remembered from their introduction. "My in-laws practically excommunicated John and me from the family last night when he let it slip we were doing gender selection for our next baby. Well, he didn't exactly let it slip. We had no choice but to borrow money from them to pay the clinic, so he had to say something. I don't know why he told them everything."

Lucinda Maybank dialed back her smile. "Money is a huge issue," she said with her forehead wrinkled in make-believe concern. She sighed and closed her eyes for a second.

Maureen sucked in a sharp breath and rattled on. "Not for John's parents. They've got plenty. It was the idea of family balancing they couldn't take. Tried to make us change our decision then and there. But we can't, not if we want to be sure of having a girl this time. Every normal pregnancy is fifty-fifty when it comes to the sex of the baby. That's why John and I decided on trying an IVF cycle to select gender. You know, screen the chromosomes in the lab to make sure only female embryos get transferred to my uterus. My mother-in-law accused me to my face of trying to create a designer baby, selecting eye color and other genetic characteristics. It was such a mean thing for her to say when all I want is a little girl to dress in pink. She tried to tell John that gender selection is illegal in the United States. But the truth is tons of couples from other countries, where it really is banned legally, travel to the U.S. for the service. They call it Reproductive Tourism. I'm serious. They honestly do call it that. And I, for one, understand why they come here. All couples should be allowed to balance their families any way they see fit."

Renee, the African American woman sitting on the other side of Maureen, leaned forward in her chair. "Stop it, Maureen," she said. "Just stop. I can't listen to you blather on about gender selection when I can't get pregnant at all. It's obscene what you're doing, and wrong, taking a cell from a five-day-old embryo trapped in a petri dish to check its chromosomes for gender, and then discarding it if it isn't what you want. No one on God's green earth can say that's moral."

Maureen flushed scarlet. She snapped back at her accuser. "You aren't informed on the subject, Renee. For your information, the American Society for Reproductive Medicine isn't against gender selection. They say individual doctors should have the right to decide for themselves if they want to offer it on their list of services, and since so many do, they must not think it's wrong, or obscene, as you say. It's the cost that's obscene, as much as twenty thousand dollars just to get started. Good thing it has a ninety-nine-point-nine percent success rate. John wouldn't have lowered himself to ask his parents for money if it weren't a sure thing...almost. And by the way, we aren't into gender selection by ourselves. The number of requests for it in the United States alone has more than doubled over the last five years. Which means you and your mother-in-law are behind the times."

❦

"Yes, sir, behind the times," said Pastor Seabrook to Gabe. "That's what I am...and embarrassed by how little I know about how doctors treat infertility. From what you said on the phone, it's frightful the choices women are facing these days. I had no idea."

Gabe rubbed his eyes, exhausted from his sleepless night at the motel. "Me, neither," he said, blinking and squinting, "not 'til I got slammed upside the head with info overload these last few weeks. Coming to see you was Charlotte's idea, Anne's sister. I bent her ear with my problems for a little while. And she wanted to help, really, but didn't know how. It's a mystery why she's still speaking to either one of us.

Anne tried to talk her into acting as a surrogate. You know what that is, right?"

"I do," said the pastor, "but only from a distance. My daughter has a friend..." He paused in thought for a second. "I hate to say this, but when my daughter told me her friend was taking money to carry someone else's baby, I found myself judging the poor girl harshly, never stopping to think she may have been the last hope for some childless couple to become parents...have a family. Besides, who am I to judge anyone? I'm just a garden variety preacher."

≼≼≼

"Ladies! Ladies, please. You have to stop judging one another." Lucinda was speaking to Maureen and Renee, whose back-and-forth rhetoric had grown too sharp to be productive. "And no more arguing about ethics. We're here to support each other...not engage in insensitivity. Maureen, your facts about gender selection are correct. And, Renee, it's okay to have a dissenting opinion as long as you remain respectful to fellow participants while expressing it. We're all tender in our feelings at this time in our lives, regardless of where we are on our journeys. We're in pain, struggling."

Brenda, the oldest woman in the group, seated on the far side of Renee, made no effort to mask her irritation. "Why do you keep saying *we*, Lucinda? You aren't struggling with anything. It's patronizing the way you talk down to us like we're children. You're younger than I am."

"Oh, Brenda, forgive me. I didn't realize I was coming across that way...trying too hard to relate, I guess. The suffering of every woman in this room is heart wrenching, palpable. Believe me, I feel deeply along with each one of you."

Nell, the pretty young participant on the far end of the row from Anne, began talking in tones so low that Anne had trouble hearing her. "I have a cousin going through gender selection, too," Nell said, "but not for family balancing like you, Maureen. She's a carrier of the gene for Fragile X Syndrome. It's a disorder that shows up mostly in boys... causes symptoms like autism and intellectual impairment. Girls can have it, too, but since boys have it more often, my cousin is selecting for a girl. Her doctors will screen her embryos in the lab for the Fragile X gene even in the females. Hemophilia is in the same category, and Tay-Sachs disease, plus a form of muscular dystrophy called Duchenne...and other conditions."

Renee, the African American woman, stopped Nell with a question. "Is sickle cell anemia on that list? I have friends who are worried to death about giving birth to a child with sickle cell. One got an abortion to avoid it. It's more common in the black community."

"Wait a minute," said Brenda, the oldest woman. "Are you saying boys who have Fragile X don't live long enough to become fathers? Is that the reason the disorder is inherited from moms?"

"Yes, usually," said Nell. "My cousin has the single gene for Fragile X, but she doesn't have the disorder herself. She's a carrier...terrified of bringing a desperately sick little boy into the world."

Lucinda interrupted this disturbing exchange of

information with an unsuccessful effort toward lightening the mood. "And I'm sure she has mixed feelings, unbearable feelings. So you see, Renee, no matter where you are personally - each of you - someone else in the infertility community is having a harder time."

After sighs of agreement within the group, Anne began telling her own story in a flat tone. "My father is terminally ill with cancer."

Nell, Brenda, Renee, Maureen, and Lucinda stared at Anne, who kept talking as if the process of unburdening facts about herself was somehow making her feel better. "I want my dad to see a grandson before he dies. He already has six granddaughters...my two sisters' children." She took a breath and blew it out in a loud sigh. "But it's looking like that's not going to happen. My husband just lost his job; we had a huge fight about money last night; he left the house; I told him to get out. We've been married three-and-a-half years without using birth control, with no baby, not even a miscarriage or chemical pregnancy. The clinic I go to calls it unexplained infertility. I wanted to start IVF this month, but Gabe, my husband, was shocked out of his mind by some of the optional procedures that can go along with it. Doesn't matter now, though. He's gone. And if that weren't enough, both my sisters are mad at me. I asked one of them to act as a surrogate, but she has health issues of her own, and it infuriated my other sister that I even mentioned the idea. So now they're both upset."

After an awkward silence, Renee said aloud what everyone else was thinking. "That all sounds about right." A morbid snicker rippled across the semicircle of despairing women.

Lucinda gave Renee a sharp look before speaking to the group newbie. "Thank you so much for sharing, Anne. That makes you one of us now."

— *Anne* —

Have you ever wished for a straightforward solution to a problem that has been driving you crazy for months...years? It was my misguided reason for trying out Lucinda Maybank's support group. I was hoping Dr. Armond had been right, that it would help me to hear how other women experiencing infertility were coping. Can you imagine how horrified I was to find out every woman in the group was worse off than I? Not one had discovered a perfect solution to her problem, only imperfect possibilities. These women needed help more than I did, and not the bogus kind Lucinda Maybank was dispensing. We all needed divine wisdom and guidance, not human expedience defined as something helpful or useful in a particular situation, though sometimes morally questionable. We needed God in our lives - God, Jesus, and the Holy Spirit - and divine Truth found in prayer and the Word.

From whence cometh my help. My help cometh from the Lord, which made heaven and earth.
PSALM 121:1B-2 KJV

But blessed is the one who trusts in the Lord, whose confidence is in him. He will be like a tree planted by the water that sends out its roots by the stream. It does not fear when heat comes; its leaves are always green. It has no worries in a year of drought and never fails to bear fruit.
JEREMIAH 17:7-8 NIV

Trust in the Lord with all your heart, and do not lean on your own understanding. In all your ways acknowledge him, and he will make straight your paths.
PROVERBS 3:5-6 ESV

Chapter

13

Pastor Seabrook stared in shock at Gabe. "Charlotte can't act as a surrogate for anyone," he said. "Her health…"

Gabe shrugged assent. "Which did not stop Anne from putting her on the spot."

Seabrook looked perplexed. "I know Charlotte…quite well, in fact…unselfish, a good mother, strong in her faith. She'd help Anne if she could, but the poor thing has had some hard knocks of her own these past few years. I'd say she's still in recovery herself."

Gabe nodded. "Charlotte and the other Yorks are all believers, like me," he said, "but Anne isn't, not really."

On that revelation from Gabe, Pastor Seabrook experienced an ah-ha moment he could not wait to share. "Unequally yoked…that's what you and Anne are. It's how the *Bible* refers to a union between a believer and a nonbeliever."

"I take the blame for letting that happen," Gabe said. "I knew before we got married Anne was estranged from God, but I convinced myself it was a phase she'd grow out of sooner or later…only she didn't."

Defeat etched lines of sadness on Gabe's face. Pastor Seabrook's dark eyes showed increasing concern for his counselee. He had good reason to be troubled. The good pastor was more aware than he wished to be of the negative dynamics in the York family. "I've known Anne and her people since she was a little girl," he said, his voice quiet. "The problem you're facing now started a long time ago. Anne's father, Nick, began deferring to her the day she was born, holding her up as deserving of special attention. And he's still doing it, even though she's an adult now. To hear Nick York tell it, no other woman in the world has ever succeeded in becoming a successful OB-GYN. It's a family dance, and every member of the York clan knows the steps."

The more the pastor spoke, the more beaten down Gabe looked. He appeared to be shrinking physically despite his youth and vitality. He dropped his head lower and lower as if drowning in humiliation. "And then there's me," he said, "the loser son-in-law who can't hang onto a job. Anne threw me out last night."

The pastor's eyes widened. "You lost your job...and left home!?"

Gabe nodded. Pastor Seabrook whistled a sigh. "This is worse than I thought. As my daughter would say, 'Bummer.'"

"Bummer...that's what infertility is!" shouted Renee, the most vocal participant in Lucinda Maybank's group. "Our marriage has gotten so bad over it, we had to sign ourselves up for counseling. My husband, Ralph, told the therapist in the very first session I wasn't the same woman he married ten years ago, that I had turned into a fanatic obsessed with my own reproductive system. Fixated is the word he used. He said he was sick and tired of my being jealous of every woman pushing a baby stroller in the mall. Then he blurted out all kinds of private stuff about our pitiful sex life that's too embarrassing to say out loud. Y'all know what the men's rooms in the clinics are about, right? They aren't restrooms, for sure."

Every woman in the group groaned and nodded as Renee continued her soliloquy. "Ralph proceeded to tell the therapist all about the men's room and how much anxiety it caused him every time he had to go in there. I felt like knocking him out of his chair."

Lucinda found herself having to wrest control of the floor from Renee, whose story was gaining warp speed. "Oh, Renee. I'm so proud of the two of you for seeking counseling," she declared. She had no choice but to resort to talking over Renee in her loudest leader-voice. Said she to the whole group, "Having a professional person validate your emotions is key. You and your husband, or partner, need reassurance you aren't alone in how you feel. It's an important function of our group, too. We've all got each other's backs here. That's a promise."

Brenda, the oldest participant, jumped in on Lucinda to begin a rant of her own, one that showed how raw her feelings were. "Why do you want to pump Renee's head full of that nonsense, Lucinda? We don't have each other's backs. Not one person in this pity party was there last week when my mother told me God was going to punish me for what I'm doing. She doesn't approve of my trying to get pregnant using in vitro with a donor egg. Never mind I'm forty-five years old and have already struck out three times with my own eggs in three different IVF cycles, miscarriages all. But Mom doesn't care about that, or the fortune this infertility thing is costing my husband and me, or the fact that she's the one who advised me to wait on having a family in the first place, *'until you get your career going,'* she said way back when. Which I did, and not because she told me to, of course, but I did wait. And this is where it's gotten me. Forty-five years old, going on forty-six, with no baby, severely limited egg reserves in my ovaries, and no more money to throw at the problem. I don't just *feel* depleted in every way. I *am* depleted in every way. And my husband is barely hanging in. This group doesn't have my back. I've never felt more alone."

Nell, the youngest and blondest woman in the group, agreed with Brenda's rant. "Brenda...Brenda...honey," she said. "You aren't the only one here who feels alone. When you think about it, every one of us is isolated and afraid, especially when the money starts running out. I read online that donor eggs cost as much as ten thousand dollars."

"Oh, yes," said Brenda. "Sometimes more. My husband and I have come to the end of what we can borrow."

"What about adoption?" Renee said in a weak effort to help Brenda see she was not out of options. "Seems like the logical next step."

Renee's suggestion made Brenda angrier. "Oh, I get it," she said. "Women like Maureen over there can buy any procedure she wants, 'cause she's got rich in-laws, right down to IVF for the sole purpose of selecting gender. While women like me, and probably the rest of you, have trouble scraping up money for procedures we actually need. It isn't fair. Neither is medical insurance. What's fair about some corporate insurance programs covering infertility procedures, while others don't, including the company I work for. I've been trying to have a baby for three years, and believe me, nothing about my journey has been fair. And nobody's got my back."

Maureen, the woman with the wealthy in-laws, spoke up, her tone making it apparent she had little sympathy for Brenda or anyone else in the group. "Maybe," she said directly to the upset Brenda, "you shouldn't have waited so long to start trying. Everybody knows the older you get, the less likely..."

Lucinda could not let such a callous remark go by without addressing it. "Maureen...Brenda knows the facts. It's her feelings she's dealing with now. Don't forget, as group members, we are committed to mutual kindness."

"Sorry," Maureen mumbled. "But you have to admit, it's obvious all of us have brought a lot of our problems on ourselves, like waiting too long to start trying."

Brenda, whose demeanor was no longer that of a calm and cool career woman, began weeping at Maureen's pronouncement. The two participants on either side of her - Nell, the sweet young blond and Renee with the elaborate braided updo - tried to comfort Brenda, while Maureen, the only one with serious financial backing, got a guilty look for attacking a fellow group member.

Renee said to the weeping Brenda as she stroked her arm, "You're right. Not one of the rest of us has enough money for all the expensive treatment choices, if knowing that helps you. Only Maureen, from her in-laws." Renee shot Maureen a scathing glance.

Blond Nell contributed her own kind words of empathy. "You're right about everything, Brenda. Billy and I had to refinance our house to raise money for treatments. We cashed out the little bit of equity we had built up."

"Well, duh," said the affluent Maureen. "We're in the same boat. Only difference is we borrowed from Bill's mom and dad instead of a bank."

"That's not borrowing," said Renee. "That's floating a loan you'll never have to pay back. What about you, *new girl?*" Renee sent Anne a blistering stare, angry at the rookie participant for no apparent reason. Anne looked shocked; Renee did not care. She kept berating her. "I guess your husband is a doctor or something...easy street."

Anne had to work at controlling herself, when what she wanted to do was punch Renee in the face. "No," she said in a quiet, though shaky voice. "I told you a minute ago. My husband lost his job this week. I'm the doctor in the family...OB/GYN."

Lucinda Maybank jumped in on the exchange before Renee had time to snap back. "Oh, dear, Anne. I forgot to tell you. We don't reveal our professions in group meetings. It has the potential to cause envy...bring out negative feelings."

"Sure does and sure did," said the unstoppable Renee. Maureen, agreeing with Renee for the first time since they had met, contributed a raucous blurt-out of her own. "Which is the reason," she exclaimed, "that I'm so glad to be a stay-at-home mom with my two boys. No woman in her right mind would be jealous of that!"

Brenda picked up her professional power-purse from the floor and got to her feet in front of her chair. She made eye contact with Maybank. "Clearly, this group is no longer for me, Lucinda. The last few times I've come here, I've left feeling worse. Best of luck to all of you. No hard feelings."

She began a determined walk toward the door. Anne, the newbie, called out to Brenda as she exited. "Brenda, wait. You never mentioned prayer. Don't you ever pray for God's mercy? I have a praying sister...two praying sisters...a whole praying family. even my husband. I'm beginning to think they're right and I'm wrong."

Brenda glanced in Anne's direction with sad eyes, then she disappeared into the darkness of the hallway. Sweet blond Nell rose and hurried after her. Anne turned around and stared wide-eyed at the two remaining participants, Renee and Maureen. "What about you?" she said to both. "Does no one around here pray? It just hit me like a lightning bolt. We all need to be down on our knees."

"I do my praying at home," said Renee. "Lucinda doesn't allow anyone to bring up religion in the group. Kind of a dumb policy now that I think about it."

Lucinda reprimanded Renee with a harsh look before addressing Anne. "We've agreed not to muddy the waters here with our various belief systems, Dr. York...Anne. Did I forget to mention that when you called?"

Anne did not back down. "You mentioned it, but I'm thinking Renee may be right...kind of a dumb policy."

Maureen jumped to Lucinda's defense. She had no intention of letting a new woman get control of the group, dysfunctional though it was. "Who do you think you are?" she said to Anne. "Coming in here all self-important, finding fault with Lucinda's rules. This is a feelings group, not a prayer meeting."

Anne looked confused. "Feelings?" she said.

Renee could not resist sticking Lucinda Maybank and Maureen with a verbal needle. "Yep," she said to Anne. "Lucinda and Maureen are high on feelings. Can't you tell?"

Maureen, angry now, defended herself to Renee. "Stop putting me in a box," she said. "You don't know me. This isn't my first go around with IVF. I've been through it twice already, years ago, before my two boys were born. It was right after the clinics had started offering egg transfer procedures to younger women. But in my case, even though I was much younger then, the doctors were able to retrieve only three eggs during each of my IVF cycles. Which terrified me that if I didn't have all three embryos transferred to my womb, I'd have less chance of one of them implanting successfully. The problem was that all three implanted both times, and since I knew I couldn't handle multiples, I elected to reduce two of them. I did that twice, intentionally, to get my boys. How am I supposed to pray about a thing like that? And what about the IVF cycle I'm in the middle of right now, when I get to the point where I have embryos in a petri dish in the lab just sitting there waiting for day five so they can be genetically screened for gender? I want a little girl so badly, so you know what that means for the male embryos. No, Renee. I don't pray, because I can't pray. I live with the pain and guilt of my decisions and keep my eye on the prize."

Maureen, the only financially secure woman in the group, also seemed the most miserable. She shifted her attention back to Anne. "Don't ever bring up prayer again," she said to her in a scorching tone. "This group is about dealing with emotions no woman should ever have to endure."

Lucinda, having lost control of the session, decided to cut and run. "I think this is an excellent stopping point for the evening," she said. "Quite a productive meeting, don't you all agree? Got lots of painful feelings out."

Nell came back into the room with a dejected look. She took her seat with a sigh. Lucinda gave her a quick update. "We've decided to close early tonight, Nell. Is Brenda all right? Did you speak with her?"

Nell answered gloomily. "She said for us not to be concerned, that she'd be okay...her work keeps her sane. She won't be back next week, though, but then neither will I."

"Oh?" Lucinda said. "I'm disappointed to hear that, Nell. I thought you were benefiting..."

"It's not the group," Nell said. "The group is fine. It's just that, well, I turned eight weeks pregnant today, and the clinic put me back under the care of my regular OB/GYN. They say I'm a success story."

"Congratulations!" said Lucinda. "That's wonderful news. I'm sure I speak for all of us when I say we're thrilled for you."

Nell smiled sweetly and brushed her fair hair away from her blushing cheeks. "Thank you," she said. "It's an answer to prayer. My whole family has been praying for me."

Renee chuckled and fixed her gaze on Anne. The two of them grinned at each other, then they said at the same time, *"That sounds about right."*

⟞⟝⟞⟝

"Prayer!" Pastor Seabrook shouted at Gabe. "It's the only thing that's going to do you any good, man. You're facing so many problems, I can't keep them all straight. Preacher platitudes like I'm used to handing out won't cut it."

Pastor Seabrook got up and walked around his desk. Then he sat in the visitor's chair next to Gabe's. "Most of this is over my head," he said. "We need to ask the Holy Spirit to help us."

Pastor Seabrook's words did not encourage Gabe. "What kind of praying is that?" he said. "Sounds weak."

For the first time in the session, the aging preacher appeared to have confidence in his knowledge of a topic. "Asking the Spirit of God to pray with you isn't weak, just the opposite. It's tapping into the most powerful force in existence. Nothing is hopeless for the Holy Spirit. You and I... we can't see all God's plans and solutions for those who love Him. We've already admitted that to each other. Now let's admit it in prayer, claim God's promise in *Romans 8:26*"... *the Spirit helps us in our weakness. We do not know what we ought to pray for, but the Spirit Himself intercedes for us through wordless groans.*

"Let's pray like that together Gabe. Dear Lord, we come to you admitting forthrightly that we don't know how to pray about the many hard things we meet along life's pathway. The only thing we know for certain to ask for in this situation is assurance concerning Anne's salvation, which seems to be in question these days. We also beg for your divine guidance with all the other problems causing Gabe and Anne to suffer. Thank you, Holy Spirit, for hearing our requests. And thank you, Father God, in the name of Jesus, for covering Gabe and me and all our families with your grace, mercy, forgiveness, and salvation as we submit our lives to you in obedience. Praise the Father, Son, and Holy Spirit! Amen."

— *Anne* —

As I try to capture in words the story of my heartache, mine and that of the other women in Lucinda Maybank's support group, I hope you don't think I'm minimizing Gabe's feelings, or any other spouse's. I see now that he felt as much pain as I did. But back then, I was deaf, dumb, and blind to it. I saw women as the only broken ones - Nell, Brenda, Renee, Maureen, and me - with the grief of infertility our common language. And though I had encountered a parade of patients in my medical practice suffering from the same condition, their sorrow did not become real to me until I experienced it myself. Until then, I considered infertility a physical problem. Not to say I wasn't aware that emotional disturbances always accompanied it. Yet I did not see them as important. My attitude toward my patients' sob stories remained callous. I wasn't a shrink, after all. When they wanted or needed to *talk, talk, talk,* I routinely sent them to a different kind of professional whose job it was to *listen, listen, listen,* never dreaming I would soon become a member of their heartsick sisterhood. My new circumstance as an advanced case of female dysfunction became official the moment I sought help from Lucinda Maybank's support group. But on dragging myself to that first session, I found a shocker awaiting me there. After listening to the other women pour out their hearts, I realized they were in worse shape than I. For the first time, I began to understand how large and varied was the community of the barren brokenhearted. And Lucinda Maybank's group was just one small cell. My heart ached for these women. I wanted to help them, but at the time, I did not know how.

[Jesus] *The Spirit of the Lord is on me, because he has anointed me to proclaim good news to the poor. He has sent me to proclaim freedom for the prisoners and recovery of sight for the blind, to set the oppressed free, to proclaim the year of the Lord's favor.*
LUKE 4:18-19 NIV

Chapter

14

Rose and her father sat in folding chairs on the dock enjoying a cool breeze. Nick's empty wheelchair had been rolled to the side and braked. An outdoor blanket, with which Nick would have nothing to do, lay abandoned in the seat. The patient was too busy baiting his hook and casting for bass to worry about getting chilled. Neither he nor Rose realized Anne was nearby until her footfalls on the upper dock gave her away.

Nick blessed his youngest daughter with his sunniest smile when he saw her striding toward him. "Annie!" he said. "What a surprise. Look-a-here, Rose. Anne is here. Pull up a chair, slugger!"

Anne pretended not to notice how disgusted Rose looked. She kissed her father's forehead and patted his thin back. Then she dragged over a faded deck chair and plopped into it.

"Catching anything?" she said to her dad.

In Anne's presence, the old man looked happier, even healthier. "Nahhh," he said. "Playing at it to get some outdoor air. Beats helping Sallie work on her thousand-piece jigsaw puzzle of Elvis in his white bell bottoms."

Anne decided to make her snotty oldest sister acknowledge her. "How're you doing today, Rosie?" she said with no sincerity. "Where're the girls...at home practicing their pageant walks?"

Rose looked pained, but she managed, as a result of lifelong practice, not to pick up Anne's bait. She let it lie there on the dock, stinkier than her father's real pile of bait. "They're with William," she said. "It's my shift with Daddy. Charlotte will be here any minute."

Anne gave no indication she'd heard one word Rose had uttered. She stared out across the inlet, blank of expression. "We're separated," she finally said.

Nick alerted. "Who's separated? From what?"

"Gabe and me."

Rose's interest heightened at Anne's bad news. Nick began spluttering. "But he was just here...Gabe...helping Manuel with the lawn."

"He's not separated from Manuel...from me," Anne said, feeding her sister's curiosity. "Gone, as in moved out. Poof."

Nick sat up straighter, indignant now. His face had returned to its sickly pallor. "Well then, tell him to move back in. This is no good."

Rose's eyebrows appeared paralyzed in two high arches. She could barely contain her joy at Anne's misfortune. Said she with inappropriate glee, "But I don't understand. Gabe is such a nice guy."

Anne shot Rose a cutting look. "So it's automatically my fault, Gabe being so nice and all?"

"If the shoe fits..." Rose said, waiting, salivating for juicy details.

Anne shut down her curiosity. "Why don't you go back to the house, Rose," she said. "Tell Mama the good news...Anne has a big old problem she doesn't know how to fix."

Rose got to her feet in a huff and stomped up the dock, stopping after six steps to throw a last verbal dart at her sister. "Everybody knows Gabe is a nice guy. This is on you."

Anne clenched her jaw. She forced herself to wait for Rose to get out of earshot before addressing her father again. Nick endured the long silence by watching a sailboat tack toward open water. He looked upset, disappointed, ill. Anne reached for the woolen blanket in the wheelchair and draped it over his lap.

Nick spoke without taking his eyes off the sailboat, not at first, anyway. "Want to talk it over?" he said to his baby girl, this after Rose's footsteps had faded away.

Anne sighed defeat. "Nothing much to say. He lost his job; I told him to leave."

"He can get another job. What's the real reason?"

"Money."

"You two ever tried living within your means? It's what worked for your mama and me. We didn't have a dime starting out, now all this." He gestured to indicate the house and grounds.

"You sound like Gabe," said Anne.

"Thank goodness one of you is talking sense. And let's get something else out on the table. Why don't you come to church with Gabe anymore, sit with the rest of us...family?"

"Because I'm not a hypocrite. I work like a dog all week and need to rest on Sundays."

"My cancer is terminal."

"Don't talk like that. If you repeat something out loud enough times, it'll manifest in your life. You said so."

"You're misquoting me. I've spoken a lot about the power of prayer in my time, but not using oddball words like manifest. No sense sugar coating things. I'm your ailing, terminally ill daddy, who has a last request of you."

"I know, I know. You want a grandson to cap off your six granddaughters."

"Well, sure, honey. It would be great to have a little boy around here, but that's not what I meant. I want you to pay a visit to Pastor Seabrook, maybe more than one, considering how overwrought you are. I don't want to go out worrying about your...situation."

"You wanted to say my sanity, didn't you? Which I'm still hanging onto for the most part, but Gabe and I as a couple are too far gone for counseling."

"I'm not talking about marriage counseling. I'm talking about for you alone. I've done everything I know how to do. Given you every advantage. And now here I am sick and dying, and all I see is you making yourself and everybody around you miserable. Rose, Gabe, Charlotte, your mother... even me. I never thought I'd ever hear myself saying such a modern thing, but you need professional help."

"Dad...Daddy. Why are you making a federal case out of this? Lots of married people get separated and divorced, end up hating each other. And lots of women are barren."

Nick took hold of Anne's forearm and insisted she make eye contact. "Will you listen to reason?" he said. "You're in a bad way, self-destructing right in front of my face. You don't have a choice. You have to find somebody who'll know how to help you."

"Dad..."

"You know I love you, Annie. The question is do you love me? We won't even address why you don't love God."

"Hopeless...Gabe and me. We don't even love each other anymore."

"That wasn't the question. The question was *do you love your father?*"

"You know I do. You and Mom and Charlotte, all the little ones, even Rose. Only I don't know how to express it."

"What about Gabe?"

"I thought I loved him. But he's gone now, so what's the use beating myself up with regret? It's too late."

Anne closed her eyes. Nick watched tears roll down her pale cheeks. He exhaled a deep sigh, his own eyes tearing up. "You said just then that you loved me. If you meant it, and I know you did, you'll go talk to Pastor Seabrook because I'm sick and can't do anything else for you. You'll go...out of love and respect for your father. And I'm praying you'll go soon. I don't have much time left, and prayer is all I have left to give you."

Anne stared out over the water. "Maybe," she said. "I'll think about it. I've already been thinking about prayer. And now you're telling me to go spill my guts to Pastor Seabrook. I have to say, those are a couple of big concepts to swallow in less than twenty-four hours."

— Anne —

I was barely able to recognize myself. Who had I turned into...
considering prayer might be a way to cope with my
problems, thinking about a visit to Pastor Seabrook for
counseling, and, most shocking of all, paying attention to
a wiser head like my father's. Never mind he was still going
down the same old religious road. I could not understand
why he would say that prayer was all he had left of value to
give me, when prayer had done nothing to help him
overcome cancer. He could not kick it, no matter how much
he, Mom, Charlotte, and Rose, plus everyone from our
church and other churches all over Savannah prayed for his
healing. How could he think God would answer his wayward
daughter's prayer for a baby? And how could I think God
might answer the prayers of Nell, Brenda, Renee, and
Maureen? I had sounded pretty confident, even to myself,
insisting in the group session that prayer was what we all
needed. Renee had sounded confident, as well. But after I got
back home and began analyzing our high-minded assertions,
my certainty began to deflate. For example, let's say the
women in the group began praying their hearts out for
children, but got no answers, or wrong answers. Or worse,
what if one or two got right answers - what they wanted -
while others did not. What, then, would be the point of all
that prayer? After all, how hard could it be for Almighty God
to give a woman a baby? Had I made a false assumption, a
false claim to the group about prayer having the power to
help? I already knew from personal experience that infertility
had plenty of negative power, enough to drive a woman to
desperate measures in a short amount of time, all to achieve
something normal. After thinking over how Dad's prayers for

healing had been denied, I began to suspect that with prayer, personal will and God's will may not line up. Did that mean making personal will the focus of one's prayers a misguided approach? I found myself ill equipped to grapple with such a possibility, not when I could feel nothing beyond my burning desire for a child. I refused to acknowledge that a better prayer on my part would have been to ask God to teach me to be grateful for whatever he chose to give me, rather than making myself miserable over something I could not get for myself. It did not take long for me to figure out that this was the way my dad conducted his own prayer life. I could also see with great clarity that it would be a healthy approach for women like Nell, Brenda, Renee, and Maureen. But I could not - *would not* - let go of the selfish idea that God might not know what was best for me, the accomplished Dr. Anne York. Does that tell you anything about who I still was, continuing to put self first as I began trying to pray again? Or, to bring it closer to home, does it tell you anything about yourself?

> *Hear my prayer, O Lord; listen to my plea! Answer me because you are faithful and righteous. I lift my hands to you in prayer. I thirst for you as parched land thirsts for rain. Come quickly, Lord, and answer me, for my depression deepens. Don't turn away from me, or I will die. Let me hear of your unfailing love each morning, for I am trusting you. Show me where to walk, for I give myself to you. Rescue me from my enemies, Lord; I run to you to hide me. Teach me to do your will, for you are my God. May your gracious Spirit lead me forward on firm footing. For the glory of your name, O Lord, preserve my life. Because of your faithfulness, bring me out of this distress.*
> **PSALM 143:1; 6-12 NLT**

Chapter 15

Late for the second time, Anne tried to make herself invisible as she slipped into the next session of Lucinda Maybank's support group. She took her same chair as before, on the end of the row next to affluent Maureen, the woman pursuing gender selection for a female baby. Group leader, Lucinda, nodded a quick greeting toward Anne without interrupting African American Renee, who now had the floor in a big way.

Renee glanced in Anne's direction, but did not stop relating her cheerless story. "And when the clinic nurse called me on Monday and said not a single one of our four frozen embryos was of high enough quality to transfer to my womb, I went to bed and stayed there forty-eight hours without getting up except to go to the bathroom and drink some water. And when my husband left for work on the third day, I found a note taped to the fridge saying he wasn't coming back. And he didn't for two nights, but on the third, he showed up at dinner time and ate a plateful of pasta with clam sauce like he'd never left."

Lucinda Maybank's reaction to Renee's account of her relationship woes was predictable. "Thank goodness he came to his senses. Some men never do. Anne, did your husband make it back home yet?"

"Nope," said Anne. "Guess he hasn't come to his senses."

Renee stifled a snigger. Maureen cut her eyes at her. "Go ahead and say it, Renee, your standard smart remark. *That all sounds about right.*"

Lucinda ignored Maureen's mean comment and continued her shallow focus on Anne. "Oh, I almost forgot to introduce you to our newest member. Anne meet Paula. Paula, meet Anne."

Paula blushed and nodded. Anne nodded back. Renee used the moment of silence to grab the floor again. "Yep," she said. "Paula is new, and the rest of us are old. What's your story, Paulie? Don't be shy. In this group, we've got each other's backs...*not.*"

Paula looked unsure. She glanced at Lucinda for permission before speaking. "We're looking to hire a surrogate in a couple of weeks," she said. "Nothing else has worked for us. IVF cycles have gotten to be too much emotionally and...well...money..."

Financially secure Maureen shuddered. "I can relate to fried emotions," she said. "My mother-in-law..."

Renee cut Maureen off. "Don't start up in here tonight about your mama-in-law, not if you don't want me to slap your face. Let's hear someone else's complaints for a change. Go on, Paula."

Paula looked at Lucinda again, who nodded for her to continue. "We - my husband and I - figured since we were going to be paying big bucks for a donor egg anyway, we may as well go ahead and ante up for a surrogate. I've had four miscarriages already with IVF using my own eggs. Can't endure another one. We'll be able to use my husband's sperm, though. The surrogate will have artificial insemination. The whole process will cost a fortune. But how else am I going to spend the money my grandmother left me? If she were still alive, she'd say go for it."

Renee leaned forward in her chair and attacked Lucinda with words. "Do you see what I mean about money in this group?" she said with acid. "Paula's got the scratch to pay for a surrogate, Maureen for an entire IVF cycle dedicated solely to gender selection, and Anne over there is a doctor. Which means she can afford whatever she wants, whether her husband comes back or not."

Anne could not let Renee's misconception go by. "I wish that were true," she said. "Doctors don't make as much as people think."

"Come on," Renee said. "You know you can get your hands on cash from somewhere. Rich aunt, rich daddy... somebody."

"You know what, Renee," Anne said. "You're right, I do have a rich daddy, but not in the sense you're talking about. My dad's rich in faith. He's a praying man, a God-fearing man, Spiritual leader of our family."

Lucinda now had the same look on her face as the week before when she'd lost control of the group. "Anne!" she barked. "Did you forget we don't talk about religion here? Or prayer? Please...refrain."

But Anne did not. She barked back louder at the group's peculiar leader. "What a load of horse manure, Lucinda. I know you're trying to be helpful. I guess you are, anyway. And you have been helpful to me in a backward kind of way. You've made me see I can't survive the trauma of infertility without God on my side."

Lucinda's nostrils flared dragon-like. "Well then, you'll have to find another group."

"Oh, I'm not just going to *find* another group. When I feel better, a little stronger, I'm going to *start* another group, one that focuses on God, with prayer as its foundation."

Renee made a wow face that morphed quickly into a huge smile. "What do you know?" she exclaimed. "Somebody finally said something that sounds right!"

— *Anne* —

I don't like having to tell you this, but I did not leave Lucinda Maybank's support group and immediately start an amazing new one "focused on God, with prayer as its foundation," reason being I wasn't able to right away, nowhere near. I was weaker and more confused than ever, still stumbling around in the terrible darkness of separation from Jesus. Even after I realized that any woman suffering from infertility needed to be down on her knees praying about it before Holy God, I still found myself incapable of engaging in humble supplications that would be pleasing to the Righteous Father in any way. In my mind, prayer was still all about my own wants. I thought I could use it as a patch to mend one part of my life without addressing the whole. The idea of giving my entire being over to God did not agree with self's desire to stay in control. And what self desired was to use the power of prayer selectively to its own ends, and since I remained a slave to self, that was what I tried to do. The best way I can explain it is this: I did begin praying, a lot, but in a hollow, self-centered manner, all because I kept clinging with a death grip to the old wineskin of my old life - *self!* - instead of replacing it with the new wineskin of an all-embracing life in Christ. No wonder I could not hear Jesus whispering his holy wisdom into my ear. I was too busy listening to the faithless screech of *self!*

> [Jesus] *No one sews a patch of unshrunk cloth on an old garment. Otherwise, the new piece will pull away from the old, making the tear worse. And no one pours new wine into old wineskins. Otherwise, the wine will burst the skins, and both the wine and the wineskins will be ruined. No, they pour new wine into new wineskins.*
> **MARK 2:21-22 NIV**

[Jesus] *If you try to hang on to your life, you will lose it.*
But if you give up your life for my sake, you will save it.
MATTHEW 16:25 NLT

Chapter

16

Anne's Jaguar (her luxury vehicle owned mostly by the bank) sat a bit less proudly in the driveway of Anne and Gabe's upscale house (also owned mostly by the bank) that she now occupied alone. When Anne had driven up, she'd been too tired to go through the process of securing her fine car in the garage. Feeling fortunate to have made it back home at all after her second unnerving visit to Lucinda Maybank's support group, she had given in to weariness and left the Jag outside.

Once in the house, she dropped her purse and keys on the staircase in the spacious foyer and shed her jacket and shoes. All she wanted was to make her way upstairs to the owner suite and hide from the world.

Her first destination in the suite was the bathroom, where she paused to gaze with dull eyes at the clutter on the counter between the twin sinks. Several used pregnancy test kits still gave evidence of her compulsion for testing. She hated those kits. Their results had stabbed her in the heart every time they'd confirmed she was not pregnant. The collection of empty boxes and their used contents were awful reminders of her torment. She stood staring at them for a couple of seconds before noticing her reflection in the vanity mirror. What she saw gave her pause. The chalk-faced, hollow-cheeked woman staring back at her had a cold, blank look. Anne recoiled and hurried out of the bathroom. She entered the closet dressing room where she changed into pajamas and a robe, leaving her street clothes in a pile on the carpet.

Tea, she thought on re-entering the bedroom, the idea of which gave her enough strength to go back downstairs and make herself a hot mug of chamomile before retreating again to the safety of her and Gabe's room.

Where she sat in silence in one of the easy chairs, brooding and gazing out the window at the streetlight across the street. Her cheeks stung from salty dried tears that had been flowing off and on all day. She felt tired and bereft of hope. Her body had become an empty vessel, her brain disengaged. It was in the vacuum of this desolate moment that something Charlotte had mentioned floated up, something Anne remembered her sister chattering about on the day she had asked her to act as a surrogate. It was the account of what had happened in the life of an *Old Testament* woman, who, like Anne, had also found herself emotionally drained over not being able to get pregnant... Hannah's story.

Anne set her mug on a side table and got up from the easy chair. Her pale cheeks gained a tinge of color as she stared at Gabe's desk against the wall. She walked over, sat down in his swivel chair, and began searching through desk drawers. When she found his *Bible,* she pulled it out and studied his name embossed in gold on the leather cover - Gabe Simmons. The *Bible,* a graduation gift from his parents when he had finished The Citadel, was now worn from much use.

Anne clutched it to her chest and closed her eyes, trying to remember the details of what Charlotte had said. "Hannah... made a vow," Anne whispered, "and God honored it and gave her a son. What was the reference? What exactly did Charlotte say?" Anne relaxed her mind in the manner she had learned how to do when performing c-sections, a technique she often relied upon to help calm her nerves and remain super alert at the same time. Her eyes popped open. "*Samuel,*" she said aloud. "*First Samuel.*"

She thumbed through Gabe's *Bible* using the reference tabs to find *First Samuel,* Chapter One, talking to herself as she scanned the verses with her forefinger. "Hannah... Hannah was desperate to have a baby, so she went to the temple to pray, and after much weeping, she made a vow before the Lord, that if He would send her a baby boy, she'd give him back into God's service all the days of his life."

Anne squeezed her eyes shut and rubbed her temple with her free hand. On blinking them open again, she stared straight ahead and spoke aloud in a determined voice, "If Hannah could make a vow before God in exchange for a son, a literal vow, then why can't I?"

She went back to the reference in *First Samuel* and continued reading and paraphrasing. "*And Hannah wept so openly that Ely, the priest, thought she was drunk in the temple, and he reprimanded her. But Hannah told him she was not drunk, but troubled and desperate. And Ely said for her to 'go in peace.' And then he asked God to grant Hanna whatever she was praying for. And she dried her eyes, and her face was no longer downcast. She went back to her husband, and in due time, God gave her a son... Samuel.*"

Anne looked up from the *Bible* and declared with hope, "All because she made a vow in prayer."

Anne thought hard another few seconds before taking a legal pad and a pen out of Gabe's desk drawer. She placed her left forefinger on the reference in *First Samuel* to keep the place, and with her right hand printed the words, *Anne's Vow Before God*, in big letters at the top of the first sheet. Then she prayed a silent prayer before recording what was in her heart.

Nightfall outside made the interior of *New Light Church* shadowy and dim. Anne, now in street clothes and carrying a tote, entered the hushed space from the vestibule doors. She looked around, checking to make sure no one else was present before walking down the aisle of the sanctuary and taking a seat at the top of the three altar steps. After a final glance about, she began unpacking her tote...ten candles, along with the same number of mismatched holders. She fitted the candles into the holders, arranged them in a half-circle just beyond the top altar step, and lit them. Their flames cast moving shadows on the walls of the sanctuary, an eerie effect.

Anne took an envelope out of her tote, kissed it, and pressed it to her heart, pausing for a quick prayer before placing it on the floor within the semicircle of burning candles. She knelt then, her hands together in ardent prayer, face earnest and upward, eyes closed, lips moving silently.

On finishing her prayer, she opened her eyes to the glow of candlelight and retrieved the envelope. Clumsily, stiffly, she got up and walked forward, positioning herself in front of the altar, where she knelt again and held the envelope up as if showing it to God on high. The envelope trembled in her hand. She tried to pray, but wept instead. Her shoulders heaved as she hung her head and bowed forward, crying audibly, openly, pitifully.

Ten minutes passed as she tried to pray, but no clear words would come, no clear thoughts, nothing rational to help her communicate on any logical level with God Almighty. Exhausted, she rose and went back to the altar steps and sat down, head in hands, still weeping, still clutching the envelope. In utter brokenness, she collapsed there on the steps, where she hid her face with her forearms. Her intent was to rest a few minutes and then try to pray again, but instead, she fell sleep.

Anne had been lying contorted and unaware across the steps for a good twenty minutes, long enough for the candles to burn partway down, by the time Berta, *New Light's* cleaning woman, came upon her. It took another five minutes for Berta to hurry off and alert Pastor Seabrook, who was even more shocked than she by the presence of an incapacitated young woman in the sanctuary. When Berta pointed toward Anne on the altar steps, the pastor stared in alarm, first at the dangerous candles, then at Anne. He approached and knelt beside her, though he did not recognize her until he brushed back her hair.

"Anne? Anne York?" he said. "What are you doing here?"

Anne tussled with the aging minister as he tried to help her sit up. Moving closer on the step, he held her tightly around her shoulders. "This isn't like you. Are you sick? On meds?"

Anne mumbled in confusion. "Spiritually sick...dying."

Pastor Seabrook let her slump against his chest. "Do you want me to call Gabe? Somebody else in your family?"

"No, no. I'll be all right. I need to go home...get some rest."

She picked up her tote and forced herself to stand. Pastor Seabrook stood also and said, "I'll check on you in the morning, if you promise to go straight home. It's late, dark out."

"I promise. Thank you, pastor. Thanks."

"Maybe I should drive you. I'm not comfortable...your leaving alone, not when you're ill like this."

"No, no. My car's out front. Lots of streetlights."

Pastor Seabrook looked unsure. "All right, I'll call you first thing."

Anne hugged him. "Thank you. Goodnight now." She walked up the aisle toward the vestibule doors, turning around a last time to acknowledge her shepherd with a weak wave. He waved back, also weakly. Concern deepened his wrinkles as he watched her exit."

Pastor Seabrook's strained look did not subside as he snuffed out the candles and began tidying up the sanctuary again. Berta, who had watched the odd exchange between the pastor and Anne from the shadows, shuffled over to help her old friend.

It was not long after he had sent Berta on her way that Pastor Seabrook spied the envelope and picked it up. In low tones, he read the words on the front. "Anne's Vow Before God." Taking the paper out of the envelope, he unfolded it and read aloud in the same quiet voice. *First Samuel 1:11* *"...and Hannah made a vow saying, 'Oh, Lord, God Almighty, if you'll only look upon your servant's misery and remember me, and not forget your servant, but give her a son, then she'll give him back to you, Lord, for all the days of his life.'"*

The pastor stopped reading for a second when he saw that the next section was a personal prayer written by Anne. He spoke those words more softly. *"Dear God, it's Anne now, begging you to hear me. Hannah prayed her prayer to you so long ago in the Old Testament. And you had mercy on her and sent her a son, Samuel. And she returned him to you after he was weaned, just as she vowed. But I'm not Hannah, God. I'm Anne in the present pleading with you to hear my prayer for a baby. My arms are empty. I'm dying of grief. If you'll give me a little boy, I'll bring him up consecrated the way Hannah brought up Samuel. I vow this before you, Mighty God. I vow!"*

— *Anne* —

If I had paid attention to the rest of Hannah's story in *First Samuel*, I may have heard God speaking to me more clearly. But I did not pay attention. I focused instead on myself. I guess I thought the pomp and ceremony I staged in the church would impress God, get his attention, make him aware of how badly I needed what I wanted. When all it did was reveal the poverty of my faith. I had forgotten, or never knew in the first place, that God hears everything because he listens, whether candles and melodrama are involved or not. The problem is that self does not listen to God. Hannah acknowledged the proper place of her own self in relation to Holy God in *First Samuel 2*, a passage made even more profound in that it foretells Jesus, *"the anointed one."* I don't know why it took me so long to follow Hannah's example.

First Samuel 2:1-10 NLT Then Hannah prayed "My heart rejoices in the Lord! The Lord has made me strong. Now I have an answer for my enemies; I rejoice because you rescued me. No one is holy like the Lord! There is no one besides you; there is no Rock like our God. Stop acting so proud and haughty! Don't speak with such arrogance! For the Lord is God and knows what you have done; he will judge your actions. The bow of the mighty is now broken, and those who stumbled are now strong. Those who were well fed are now starving, and those who were starving are now full. The childless woman now has seven children, and the woman with many children wastes away. The Lord gives both death and life; he brings some down to the grave but raises others up. The Lord makes some poor and others rich; he brings some down and lifts others up. He lifts the poor from the dust and the needy from the garbage dump. He sets them among princes, placing them in seats of honor. For all the earth is the Lord's, and he has set the world in order. He will protect his faithful ones, but the wicked will disappear in darkness. No one will succeed by strength alone. Those who fight against the Lord will be shattered. He thunders against them from heaven. The Lord judges throughout the earth. He gives power to his king; he increases the strength of his anointed one (Jesus)."

Chapter

17

After her candlelit scene at *New Light,* Anne drove home and fell into bed, where she slept better than she had in months, despite missing Gabe. She did not wake until the next morning when sunbeams streaming through the bedroom window passed over her face. She sat up, still groggy, still depressed. Her cell phone rang in her hand as she was checking the time. Pastor Seabrook's name popped up.

"Hi there. Good morning," she said. She waited, giving him a chance to speak before responding: "How am I doing? Let's see. I'm alive and awake. Those are good things, I suppose. Sorry for last night, falling asleep with those candles burning. It won't happen again."

Anne let another four seconds tick by while the kind pastor pressed her to come to his office for a chat. She had no strength left to put up roadblocks. He mentioned her father's concern. "You talked to my dad?" she said. "Oh, I get it. You two are double-teaming me now. All right, I surrender. I'll come in later this morning if that works for you." She glanced at her bedside clock. "It's ten now. How about eleven thirty?"

She paused a last time for him to agree, after which she said a polite goodbye and clicked off her phone, whereupon she experienced an abrupt drop emotionally. Talking with

Pastor Seabrook had provided a temporary balm for her battered heart, but tears came in a new flood after the conversation ended. They rolled down her cheeks and dripped off her chin as she prayed in desperation. "Oh, Jesus, help me...please," she cried out in the empty room. "I can't handle this alone anymore. Do you hear me, God?"

❧❧❧

Anne stood in the hallway outside the door to the infant nursery at *New Light Church*. She looked melancholy and pale as she stared at the poster taped to the door, a sweet print of a sleeping baby with the caption: *Shhh, little ones napping.*

Anne summoned her strength and entered the nursery. Inside the room, Berta, the cleaning woman from the night before, was making herself useful by wiping down the changing tables with disinfectant. Berta eyed Anne with suspicion. Anne offered her a wan smile and a quiet hello. The woman did not return her greeting. She rushed out of the nursery. Her reaction did not surprise Anne. She had a vague memory of Berta's presence in the sanctuary the night before.

Alone now with the baby paraphernalia, Anne moped about, looking at this, touching that. She picked up a funny old teddy bear and cuddled it, which made her feel weary. Shuffling over to one of the rocking chairs, she sat down and began rocking the bear and herself.

Pastor Seabrook entered without her hearing. He watched her from behind for a few seconds before taking a seat in the adjacent rocker. Anne acknowledged him with a slight chin dip. She showed no embarrassment about being caught

156

rocking a teddy bear.

Pastor Seabrook glanced around the sweet room before speaking. "Been a while since I was in here," he said, "not since I became a widower. My daughter is grown now, got little ones of her own."

Anne sighed and nodded to her lifelong pastor. He looked so much older to her now, and more distinguished than when she was a child. Must be the gray hair, she thought, then she said aloud, "Guess the cleaning woman who doubles as security around here told you that I was trespassing again. What's she afraid of...I might start a fire?"

Pastor Seabrook chuckled. "Now don't go being hard on Berta. She's a bit skittish, that's all. Stumbled across a burglar in the sanctuary a couple of weeks ago. Had to beat him about the head and shoulders with her mop handle to make him leave. I never even got a chance to share the Gospel with the poor guy."

Anne smiled. "He was the one in danger, not...what did you say her name was? Berta? Guess I haven't been to church enough lately to get to know her."

It was Pastor Seabrook's turn to chin dip. Anne drew in a breath and exhaled a sigh. Looking down at the teddy bear, she pretended to make him more comfortable in her arms. Her sloping shoulders revealed how fatigued she was. So did the weakness in her voice.

"I haven't been in the nursery since I graduated to the toddler room," she said. "What are those speakers for...on the wall up there?"

Pastor Seabrook looked disgusted. "For volunteers to listen to the service going on in the sanctuary if they want to, which

I'm sure they don't. It was one of those ideas that sounded good in a committee meeting but didn't pan out in real life. Sort of like the misguided idea you had when you were nine years old on how to improve Communion. Do you remember?"

"No, but I've got a feeling you're going to remind me."

"You wrote me a letter suggesting we start serving benne wafers for the Lord's supper instead of those stale old soda cracker chips. You allowed as how it might improve attendance."

"Same old know-it-all me. I'd forgotten about that."

"I didn't. Still got the letter. I can see why you would forget, though, after adult life set in with a vengeance."

"Adulting is tough. I don't ever recall feeling this bad. Seems like the more I pray, the worse I feel. Not that I've been praying for long this time around. I suppose a few days don't count for much, but it hasn't helped."

"Good thing we Christians don't live on feelings," said the pastor. "God's grace alone is sufficient, and prayer is our connection to God Himself. Emotions one way or another don't change either of those things."

"Funny you should mention emotions. I've participated in a couple of ridiculous support group sessions lately. Wallowing around in emotions seems to be the main activity, while prayer, even the mention of it, gets shoved under the rug."

"Typical these days. Lots of modern folks deny the importance of a personal relationship with Jesus. Oftentimes, even people who do pray regularly don't see that aligning their lives with God's will is the most important thing, not indulging in a bunch of selfish carrying-on before the Master. I suppose we all fall into that category at some time or another. And when we do, we have to pick ourselves up, dust ourselves off, and start over."

Anne smirked. "Did the committee who voted to install those speakers pray about it?"

"If they had, the whole idea may not have sunk like…"

Anne smirked. "…like a hammer? That cliché didn't come from the *Bible*, pastor."

The kind man grinned at Anne and shifted sideways in his seat to make direct eye contact. "You're right. But there is one instance in the Word when a hammerhead floated by a miracle," he said. "But let's stick with a more familiar reference about who's in charge of our lives, including our prayer lives: *Proverbs 19:21 NIV Many are the plans in a person's heart, but it's the Lord's purpose that prevails.*"

Anne closed her eyes, trying to muster the strength to share her pain with Pastor Seabrook. When she opened them, tears spilled over. "Plans in my heart are bringing disaster after disaster. I don't know which train wreck to address first."

He patted her arm. "Something tells me, since we're sitting here together in rocking chairs…"

"Gabe and I are separated."

"I heard that this morning."

"Who from?"

"Gabe himself, your dad, your mom, Charlotte."

"You're kidding me. Why didn't they put it on

Facebook?" She paused, thinking. "Rose probably did."

Another pause. "They warned us at the fertility clinic that lots of couples run into marital difficulties...you know, when they can't have a baby."

"Understandable."

"But in our case, infertility isn't the root problem. *I'm* the root problem."

"Can't be all you, Anne. It takes two to tango, another of my non-Biblical clichés."

"Oh, it's me all right in every way. Gabe Simmons has had his head on straight his whole life. I'm the self-centered one."

"Says who?"

"Says everybody. Gabe, Rose, Mama, a little Mexican girl out in the West End near Pooler. I tried to bargain her baby away from her."

"And what does God think about all this? Every now and then he thumps us on the shoulder to get our attention."

"Let's put it this way. He didn't thump me. He tasered me to the ground."

"So, you haven't stopped believing in God. Gabe's under the impression..."

"I've always believed. I only said I didn't to show off because I'd never run up on a situation I couldn't manage on my own, with Daddy's help, of course. He's the one I've been trying to please since I was a little girl, not God. But that was a warped lie, too. All I've really been doing is pleasing myself...running after attention fixes, grabbing for praise and congratulations on my fabulous achievements...my never-ending wonderfulness, as Rose would say."

Pastor Seabrook furrowed his brow, almost bristling. "Don't be so hard on yourself. Everybody needs a pat on the back now and then. You've worked like a good soldier all your life. It's not a bad thing to enjoy recognition, as long as you don't get to be a junky for it. But let's put all that aside and talk about what's hurting you in the present. I've been doing some reading on infertility, a complicated issue."

Anne looked at the ceiling, trying hard not to start crying again. "And now I have to deal with a preacher who reads." she said. "Spare me, please."

"Don't give me extra credit. I didn't read enough to call myself an expert."

Anne shuddered. "I'm a casualty, not an expert. Infertility is a cruel companion. And it's worse when you throw it on top of everything else...Dad's cancer; Gabe leaving; Charlotte acting like she's afraid of me; Rose and that little Hispanic girl out in Pooler hating my guts; the bank breathing down mine and Gabe's necks for payments we can barely make; not to mention that this ratty teddy bear is the closest I've ever come to having a baby. Shall I go on?"

"Sounds to me like you've got some apologizing to do in various sectors...except to the teddy bear. He doesn't look offended."

Anne smiled with no humor. "Yep, I've got people all over town who'd like to crack me over the head."

"When do you plan to start straightening things out?"

"Day time is the right time, I suppose."

"You're aware that all folks you've hurt might not buy into your apologies...right? It could take years for some people to forgive you, if ever."

"You mean I'm not going to be congratulated for my change of heart? No recognition? I thought I'd be named the most outstanding sinner-turned-righteous-glory-hog who ever existed and then presented with a trophy."

Pastor Seabrook laughed. "You need to stop talking so we can pray about this together. Then you can start making a list of injured parties you need to call on...with a humble spirit, I feel the need to add."

Anne rolled her eyes and dropped her head to her chest. After a moment, she focused her resolve. Still holding the teddy bear, she turned to face her wise pastor and held out her free hand. He took it and enveloped it in his own. Anne looked into his eyes with gratitude.

"Apologies can be empty," she said. "I know that. The few apologies I've made in my life have been insincere."

Pastor Seabrook patted her hand. "But this time, since you're going to pray with me for Jesus to be in the driver's seat, there's hope for the hopeless."

Anne smiled weakly and nodded. "I'm thankful he's willing to take me back. I don't deserve it. I don't deserve anything, especially forgiveness. That's why I want to thank God in Jesus for forgiving me anyway. *This is Anne here, God. Are you listening?*"

She clamped her eyes shut and continued the prayer she had just begun. *"Please, Father, in the name of Jesus, forgive me for behaving so selfishly. I want to stop living like that. I want my life to reflect you. Thank you for grace, your generous grace that you provided through the sacrifice of your Son."* She opened her eyes and addressed Pastor Seabrook through more tears. "Pastor, pray with me. I want to stop stumbling around and get in step with God."

Pastor Seabrook placed a hand on Anne's bent shoulder and closed his eyes. *"Father God...Anne and I come to you with all gratitude for your love, mercy, forgiveness, grace, and salvation. Thank you, Jesus, for the sacrifice you made on the cross to save our souls. Fill Anne and me now with your Holy Spirit and help us remain in step with you. In your loving name we pray. Amen."*

— *Anne* —

I don't know if Pastor Seabrook realized it, but that day in the church nursery was the first time I had ever thought about asking God to help me get in step with him, rather than imploring him to get in step with me. Which did not go along with my worldly idea that if God would listen to me and do my bidding, I'd finally be happy. I had not yet come to understand his fundamental Truth...that I would be a million times more fulfilled in life if I aspired to finding God's will, instead of focusing on self's will. Thus, my new prayer goal was to succeed at getting God to listen to me by being "good" in his presence. Maybe, I thought, my goodness would make him want to grant my will. I forgot that any actions on my part considered good by the world's standards would be filthy rags in the sight of Holy God. I also forgot about the real meaning of his grace. Jesus sacrificed everything on the cross, even his blood, all to cover me with his righteousness since I had none of my own. Then he gave me the gift of grace. All I had to do was have faith in him, faith itself being another of his grace-gifts. It was ridiculous for me to think my own inadequate goodness could be worthy of anything. My new misguided intention was to try to walk with God no matter if the effort made me miserable. I would make the sacrifice, because I was going to be good now, extra good to the purpose of getting what I wanted through prayer. Do you notice I was still after what *self* wanted, not what God wanted, as if what God wanted would be dreadful, and what *self* wanted would be great? That was a massive point to miss in my Spiritual journey, but miss it, I did, reason being I was *so very busy* trying to be *so very good*, all the while ignoring God's teaching that true goodness originates with him alone, not me and not you. Who did I think I was? Don't answer that. I already know. I remained a slave to *self*.

All of us have become like one who is unclean, and all our righteous acts are like filthy rags; we all shrivel up like a leaf, and like the wind our sins sweep us away.
ISAIAH 64:6 NIV

If we live by the Spirit,
let us also keep in step with the Spirit.
GALATIANS 5:25 ESV

But because of his great love for us, God, who is rich in mercy, made us alive with Christ even when we were dead in transgressions—it is by grace you have been saved. And God raised us up with Christ and seated us with him in the heavenly realms in Christ Jesus, in order that in the coming ages he might show the incomparable riches of his grace, expressed in his kindness to us in Christ Jesus. For it is by grace you have been saved, through faith—and this is not from yourselves, it is the gift of God—not by works, so that no one can boast. For we are God's handiwork, created in Christ Jesus to do good works, which God prepared in advance for us to do.

EPHESIANS 2:4-10 NIV

Chapter

18

Anne, still pale and weak, struggled with the effort of pushing the metal posts of a homemade sign into the ground – *For Sale by Owner*. As she worked, Gabe pulled up in his truck and parked at the curb to watch her. He let down the passenger window before switching off the engine. Leaning toward the open window, he asked, "Were you going to tell me about this or let me read it in the newspaper?"

"Change is in the air," Anne answered brightly, though her countenance was anything but shiny.

"I thought you'd call your dad to bail you out again, only this time he'd be bailing us both out."

"The old Anne would have done exactly that," she said. "The new Anne is trying to do the right thing. And it isn't right to be living in a house we can't afford."

Gabe looked suspicious. He killed the engine, got out of his truck, and walked over to where Anne was standing. After examining the pitiful sign, he gripped its edges and drove the posts deeper into the ground, which straightened the amateur sign to a respectable angle.

"Thanks," said Anne. "And by the way, selling the house isn't the only change around here. I'm cleaning up the rest of our financial mess. Come see." She started toward the garage and motioned Gabe to follow. He stood behind her as she entered the security code door on the keypad. Up went the garage door and up went Gabe's eyebrows when he saw what was inside. He took a few steps forward to get a closer look at the rusty used Ford parked in the Jag's old spot.

"Traded down," Anne said. "No payment on this one."

Gabe closed one eye to inspect the clunker. "Can't beat that. But you might be looking at a few repair bills in the near future."

"Which will get paid in cash," said the wife Gabe was having trouble recognizing.

Gabe raised the hood of the Ford and poked around the engine. He stepped back and brushed his hands off on his pant legs, giving Anne a questioning look in the process. "Are you serious about all this? Not just a whim?"

"Oh, yeah. I want to rent a farmhouse somewhere out in the country, by myself if I have to...if you can't take being around me anymore. I just want to work, pay the bills, and help Mama and my sisters with Daddy."

Gabe stepped nearer Anne and took her in his arms. "I don't care if we live in a rabbit box," he whispered as he nuzzled her ear, "as long as we're together. 'Whither thou goest...'" He paused, holding her, enjoying the physical closeness of his wife, the only woman he had ever loved. "Guess we still have some issues to work through, though... like the clinic. Main thing is we stick together."

"Oh, Gabe, please. Don't talk about the clinic, not now," she whimpered. "My heart can't take it. Hug me a little while longer. I've missed you so much."

"I like the sound of that," he murmured, cuddling her, stroking her hair. "We'll deal with that other stuff later, whenever you feel up to it."

"Thank you. I love you so much."

"Me, too, you, Annie. Me, too, you."

— *Anne* —

Okay, now that you have observed me in my new role as goody-good Annie, do not let my change in attitude fool you. And above all, don't forget...I was still operating under the notion that the fundamental reason for being good and doing good was to garner blessings from God. I wanted a baby boy so much that I was willing to do anything to get God on my side, to include throwing a lot more than a Hannah-inspired vow into the bargaining process. I was willing to behave better all around, to my own benefit, of course, like some reformed drunk who expects to be congratulated and rewarded for making the decision to stop abusing alcohol, when she should never have been abusing alcohol in the first place. Which brings me back to my greedy old *"frenemy,"* self. Truth? My new and improved behavior was as much oriented toward the wants of self as my bad behavior was, and worse when you analyze it in the context of my attempt to use contrived goodness as commerce with the Almighty. Quid pro quo. This for that. Give a little, get a lot. Which in no way reflects how God's economy works. Somewhere along the way, I had missed the point that for a Christian, doing good has to be for the glory of God alone if it is to be acceptable to him, and most certainly *not* as a tool for bartering. I had missed so many Spiritual Truths by this point in my journey that today I'm brought to my knees in gratitude that God was not then - and still is not! - finished sanctifying me in his image.

[Paul] *So whether you eat or drink or whatever you do,*
do all for the glory of God.
1 CORINTHIANS 10:31 NIV

[Jesus] *You are the light of the world. A city set on a hill*

cannot be hidden. Nor do people light a lamp and put it
under a basket, but on a stand, and it gives light to all in
the house. In the same way, let your light shine before
others, that they may see your good works and give
glory to your Father who is in heaven.
MATTHEW 5:14 ESV

[Paul] For by grace you have been saved through faith.
And this is not your own doing; it is the gift of God, not as
a result of works, so that no one may boast. For we are his
workmanship, created in Christ Jesus for good works, which
God prepared beforehand, that we should walk in them.
EPHESIANS 2:8-10 ESV

[Paul] But when the kindness and love of God our Savior
appeared, he saved us, not because of righteous things we
had done, but because of his mercy. He saved us through the
washing of rebirth and renewal by the Holy Spirit, whom he
poured out on us generously through Jesus Christ our Savior,
so that, having been justified by his grace, we might become
heirs having the hope of eternal life. This is a trustworthy
saying. And I want you to stress these things, so that those
who have trusted in God may be careful to devote
themselves to doing what is good.
These things are excellent and profitable for everyone.
TITUS 3:4-8 NIV

[Twenty-four Elders in Heaven] Worthy are you, our
Lord and God, to receive all glory and honor and power,
for you created all things, and by your will
they existed and were created.
REVELATION 4:11 ESV

Chapter

Anne knocked on the front door of Rose's home and fidgeted while she waited for an answer. She had just reached up to knock again, when the door opened, revealing Rose with her youngest offspring on her hip and next youngest clinging to her leg. Rose's makeup-free face registered surprise and confusion at seeing Anne standing there. Her initial reaction was to look beyond her younger sister to determine if she were alone.

Puzzled, then fearful, Rose blurted out her first concern. "What are you doing here? Is it Daddy?"

Anne answered quickly. "He's fine. I came over to see *you*...talk with *you*."

Suspicion replaced fear in Rose's eyes, yet she opened wide the door and ushered Anne inside.

Anne, now a guest in Rose's kitchen, watched her sister manage somehow to fill two mugs with coffee while balancing one child on her hip and crooning to the second child still clinging to her skirt. Anne remained quiet, marveling at Rose's skill at multi-tasking, wondering if she herself would ever be the mother Rose was, observing with interest when a middle-aged woman she had never seen before entered the room and took over the baby and the small skirt clinger.

"Thanks, Molly," Rose said to the woman, adding, "This is my sister, Anne." Then to Anne, "Molly is our helper. She's been with us since Daddy got worse and I had to start relieving Mom more."

Anne turned on the charm for Molly. "Hi," she said. "Looks like you've got your hands full there."

Molly nodded and smiled. She departed with dispatch, both children in tow. Anne cocked her head at Rose. "I didn't know you had a nannie," she said.

Rose opened the fridge and got out a carton of half-and-half. "Not a nannie, a mother's helper. We have five little girls, remember? And with William traveling so much for his work, I had to hire outside help, mostly because of Daddy's condition."

Anne took a slow look around Rose's tasteful kitchen. "I don't remember the last time I was in your house...way too long."

"I've never been in your house, not once. Heard in my *Bible* study group it's a real showplace, like on TV."

Anne laughed. "Yeah, showy, like it's owner. We put it on the market yesterday. If anybody in your group wants a celebrity crib, tell them to call."

Rose dismissed Anne's remark and got down to business. "What do you want?" she said. "If you think I'm going to be your surrogate, the answer is no."

"Why do you hate me so much, Rose?"

Rose bristled. "Just because I don't fall at your feet like

everyone else doesn't mean I hate you. We have an honest relationship, you and I. You're open with your opinions; I'm open with mine. For example, I feel certain the only thing you enjoy in life is acting superior. Every day you get up and ask yourself...*who can I lord it over next? Who I can make envious?*"

Anne flinched, then looked hurt. "Is that what you think of me? I'm so sorry."

"That's what everybody thinks, only they don't bother saying it. They avoid you."

Anne inhaled and let the air out slowly. She stared into her coffee mug, searching for words. "I went to see Pastor Seabrook this morning," she said without looking up. "Prayed with him, asked God for forgiveness, rededicated my life to Jesus."

Rose looked out the window, disgust contorting her features. "Fabulous," she said, "and utterly predictable. I told Mama you'd do it eventually. Now I know why you came over. You want me to organize a parade in your honor, for wonderful Anne York, the most humble servant in God's Kingdom. Thanks, but no thanks."

Anne's willingness to take Rose's insults shriveled. "You're not perfect, either," she said. "You've got no feeling for women like me, who can't get pregnant no matter how hard they try, and you sitting here all smug in your big fine house with five healthy children and a loyal husband. And you don't mind hurting Charlotte, either, about Little Annie having Down's."

Rose's attitude hardened to granite. She set down her mug and braced her hands on the counter top. She forced herself not to shout, though her left cheek twitched. "Since we're

175

both being honest today," she said in a low quaver, "I've got another bone to pick with you, your extremist involvement in IVF. It's the worst thing you've done yet. The idea of discarding embryos is despicable."

"There you go again, judging thousands of desperate women who've had their hearts broken over being infertile. How can you do that, knowing how badly they suffer from wanting children, needing children, and you here with a houseful?"

"I don't sit in judgment of all women, just you. I think God has a reason for not giving you a baby. You don't deserve a baby."

Anne flinched again. She looked sick, faint. Tears welled in her tired eyes. "I came here to apologize for hurting you," she said, "but I think Daddy has hurt you more, focusing on me all the time, burning me to a cinder under his terrible magnifying glass, all because he and Mom never had a boy. I've had to act like a boy my whole life to please him." She stopped for a second, working her hands together to stay in control. "It's not easy finding out your parents aren't perfect, just two more sinners saved by grace."

"Words are cheap," said Rose. "Seems to me you're using a different tactic to get what you think you deserve, trying to manipulate God now."

"Wow...with you as my judge, I'll never need to go to court. Handcuff me. Flog me." She waited for another nasty retort from Rose, but when none came, she tried to go down the apology road again, the reason for her visit in the first place. "Look, I came to tell you how sorry I am for causing you pain over the years. I never realized how much.

Anyway, I regret my sins. But now I'm wondering...do you regret yours?"

Rose glared at Anne, who could not bear her sister's cold silence. "You're family, Rose," she said. "I need you."

Rose refused to soften. "Words are cheap," she said again. "So are insincere apologies."

— *Anne* —

When I left Rose's house, I drove to the nearest strip mall and parked in a shady spot to sit and think. Rose had called me out in plain words on my motives for trying to please God, and I had defended myself by pointing out her shortcomings. Was that a blatant attempt to muddy the waters, attacking Rose to make my own failings seem less offensive? I gave myself a brain ache straining to make sense of things. How could turning my life around be wrong? I tried to pray. "Lord, Lord...hear me. *Is it possible Rose can see through me in ways I can't see through myself? Are my motives purely selfish? Please, Father-Jesus-Spirit, show me how to be unselfish, only don't make me stop wanting a baby. How could a normal desire like that be wrong? I know what I want from you, God, but I don't know what you want from me. If trying to please you isn't good enough to make you willing to bless me with a child, what is? Help me! I'm confused!*"

> Jesus replied: "Love the Lord your God with all your heart and with all your soul and with all your mind. This is the first and greatest commandment. And the second is like it: 'Love your neighbor as yourself.' All the Law and the Prophets hang on these two commandments."
> MATTHEW 22:37-40 NIV

Chapter

20

Manuel and his extended family were in the middle of a barbecue when Anne, driving Gabe's crew cab truck, pulled into Manuel's mobile home driveway. She got out and waved a greeting to him at the grill. Manuel smiled and waved back. But when his sister, Maria, recognized Anne, she grabbed her child, ran to the front door of the double-wide, and disappeared inside. Anne noticed Maria's swift departure, but she did not let the girl's negative reaction interrupt the objectives of her visit, which began with hefting three large shopping bags from the back seat of the truck. Manuel hurried over to help her. Anne waited for him to deposit the bags in a lawn chair, then she pointed to the bed of the truck that was loaded with large boxes packed with parts and pieces for an outdoor play set. Colorful pictures of climbing toys and a slide for small children made it plain what was inside the cartons. Manuel shouted to his brothers in Spanish, who were delighted to begin the unloading process.

Anne gave Manuel and his wife friendly hugs before getting down to the actual reason for her unannounced visit. "I came to talk to your sister, Manuel. Do you mind asking her to come outside for a minute? Her name is Maria, right?"

Manuel's happy expression turned cloudy. "Maria no want to talk to you, no give her little one away. She's hiding from you."

He gestured toward the trailer. Anne saw the window blinds snap shut. She shrugged. "I know. I saw her run for cover when I drove up. Listen, I'm not here to try to take her baby. All I want is to tell her how sorry I am for frightening her the night of your party. I want to apologize."

"She's still frightened."

Anne nodded. "Okay then, how about I go inside and reassure her. Would that work?"

"No, no," Manuel said, waving his hands nervously. "You stay here. I'll go get her." Head down and shoulders slumped, he strode with reluctance toward his front door.

⊰⊰⊰⊰

Anne walked over to a folding chair on the lawn and sat down to wait. She watched a young mother pushing her child on a tire swing. Other women bustled around picnic tables in preparation for the outdoor meal. They gave Anne sidelong glances as they worked. Children stood by in a little lineup, watching with anticipation as the chattering men assembled the new play set.

Fifteen long minutes passed before Manuel, Maria, and her little boy emerged from the mobile home and approached Anne. Maria clutched her child's hand and looked fearful as they crossed the lawn. Manuel spoke to her in a steady stream of Spanish as he seated her next to Anne. Then he sat down in a lawn chair across from the two women to act as translator/peacemaker.

Anne picked up one of the shopping bags and began

pulling out items one by one...new clothes for Maria's little boy, a toy truck, a blanket emblazoned with lightning bolt graphics, and several dinosaur picture books. Maria did not appear to like anything Anne showed her. She rose and attempted to flee, but Manuel stopped her.

Anne held up another outfit. "Manuel, tell her these things are gifts. I'm not after her child."

Manuel reassured his sister again in Spanish and pointed to the play set his brothers were assembling on the lawn. He picked up the second shopping bag and handed it to Maria. She took it and reached for the third bag. He gave it to her, nodding with relief that she wanted it.

"She understands now," Manuel said to Anne. "She likes the gifts you brought."

Anne smiled. She took a small Spanish edition of the *Bible* from her pocket and presented it to Manuel. He held up the *Bible* for Maria to see. Displeased, she cut her eyes at Anne.

Manuel tried to make up for his sister's hostility. "Thank you, thank you," he said to Anne. "You have done enough. You and Maria are friends now."

Maria's unpleasant expression contradicted Manuel's claim that all was well, but Anne decided to test her limits. "Do you think she'd let me hold her little boy?"

Manuel spoke in clipped Spanish to Maria, who responded with a fierce *no*.

Anne put her hands up in surrender. "That's good. We're all good here. No problem." She took the *Bible* from Manuel, flipped through it to find a specific picture, and held it up to show Manuel and Maria. Maria relaxed on seeing the beautiful image of the virgin Mary holding baby Jesus. She touched the picture and looked at Anne with softer eyes. And though still tentative, she reached out and touched Anne's hand.

— Anne —

Something odd happened when Maria laid her hand on mine. A feeling of tranquility washed over me the likes of which I had never experienced before, a sense of peace that let me know the Holy Spirit was in our midst. Grateful, I got back into the truck to leave, whereupon another odd progression of feelings bubbled up. I found myself thinking about Maria and her little boy instead of myself. Questions raced through my mind. What else could I do to be of help to them? Were there other material things Maria might need to take proper care of her child? Would she allow someone like me to drive her to a mall for some funded shopping? I realized with a jolt how unlike me this way of thinking was. Unless lightning struck, Maria would never be able to do anything to repay me. And yet, here I was with a desire in my heart to help her, minister to her and her little boy...an irresistible desire. And then I remembered the prayer I had prayed on leaving Rose's house: Lord, Lord, hear me. Is it possible Rose can see through me in ways I can't see through myself? Are my motives purely selfish? Please, Father, show me how to be unselfish, only don't make me stop wanting a baby. How could a normal desire like that be wrong? I know what I want from you, but I don't know what you want from me. If trying to please you isn't good enough to make you willing to bless me with a baby, what would be? Help me, Lord. I'm trying to hear you.

[God] *And I will give you a new heart, and a new spirit I will put within you. And I will remove the heart of stone from your flesh and give you a heart of flesh. And I will put my Spirit within you and cause you to walk in my*

statutes and be careful to obey my rules.
EZEKIEL 36:26-27 ESV

[Paul] *So I say, let the Holy Spirit guide your lives.*
Then you won't be doing what your sinful nature craves.
GALATIANS 5:16 NLT

Chapter

21

Nick dozed in a lounge chair under the lush canopy of live oaks that shaded the York backyard. Rose supervised her three oldest little girls as they pretended to play badminton on their grandparents' lawn. Sallie clipped day lilies and dropped them into a basket held by Charlotte. Anne stepped into this idyllic family scene through the terrace doors off Sallie's kitchen. She was carrying yet another shopping bag, which she set down on the glass top of the umbrella table.

Charlotte's expression went from relaxed to tense on seeing Anne. Sallie's look also changed, although practice over many long years made it possible for her to take on the role of mediator in an instant. She placed the shears in the basket next to the clipped flowers, pulled herself together with a shake of her shoulders, and led Charlotte by her stiff hand over to Anne at the table. Sallie handed the basket of cut lilies to Charlotte and gave her a behave-yourself look. Then she welcomed Anne with her usual motherly warmth. "Annie, darling, we're all so glad you came by." She directed a second pointed look in Charlotte's direction before gushing onward. "Imagine it! All three York sisters at home together on a weekday. Warms my heart. I'm good-a-mind to wake up your daddy."

"Don't, Mom," Anne said, studying Charlotte's pale face

and then glancing toward the middle of the lawn at Rose and her daughters. "He looks tired. Let him sleep." She paused before addressing Charlotte, exposing her case of nerves by arranging and rearranging the position of the shopping bag on the table. "Hi, Charlotte," she finally said, dry-mouthed. She swallowed with difficulty and went on. "I made a couple of things in Gabe's workshop for you and Mom and Rose."

Sallie clapped her hands together at the idea of gifts. "Rosie," she shouted to her oldest on the lawn, "get those girls of yours some popsicles out of the freezer so they'll be satisfied a few minutes. Hurry on up here. Anne's brought presents."

Disgusted by all the falderol, Rose took her own sweet time obeying her mother.

❦

Rose's little ones relaxed on the lawn eating huge popsicles, while their mother, grandmother, and two aunts sat together around the umbrella table on the terrace. Rose looked disgruntled, Charlotte fearful, Sallie nervous, and Anne so keyed up that she appeared close to tears. Sallie tried to mitigate the tension with fake gaiety. "What did you bring us, Annie?" she said. "I can't wait another second."

Anne pulled three wooden plaques from the shopping bag. She set one down at her own place and handed off the other two to Rose and Charlotte, squirming as she waited for them to read the *Bible* verse in wood-burned script. "I made them myself with Gabe's tools," she said. "The verse reminded me of us...three sisters."

Charlotte and Rose remained silent as they processed the

moment. Sallie could not bear the vacuum. "Give me yours, Anne," she said. "I want to see."

Anne handed the plaque to Sallie, who read the verse aloud. "*A person standing alone can be attacked and defeated, but two can stand back-to-back and conquer. Three are even better, for a triple-braided cord is not easily broken. Ecclesiastes 4:12.*"

The genuinely touched mother pressed the plaque to her chest and looked heavenward. "Oh, my. That's the sweetest thing - you three girls - a triple-braided cord for Jesus. I hope you made one of these for me."

"That one is mine. It matches Charlotte and Rose's. I made a different one for you."

Anne took the fourth plaque out of the bag and quoted the verse on it as she placed it in her mother's hands. "*Proverbs 31:28 Her children arise up, and call her blessed; her husband also, and he praiseth her.*"

Anne gave Sallie a moment to gaze at the script, then she added in a quivery voice, "It's who you are, Mom. Maybe Rose and Charlotte and I can be virtuous women someday, like you."

Sallie's face glowed. "I'm overwhelmed, honey. This is going straight on my breakfast nook wall so I can look at it every morning while I'm having my coffee. Thank you, Annie. No one has more creative talents than you..." She stopped talking when Anne lowered her head and began sobbing in silence, her shoulders shaking.

"Anne, sweetheart, are you all right? What's wrong? Are you ill?"

Anne squeezed her eyes shut tighter and gripped the edge

of the table. She held her breath and wiped her eyes. Rose and Charlotte exchanged glances.

"Mom," Anne squeaked out, "you have to stop talking like that. I don't want you congratulating me for making these cheap, ugly plaques. I came here to apologize to Charlotte for what I asked her to do. I need her forgiveness."

The stunned Charlotte looked back and forth between her weeping sister and stricken mother. She then looked at Rose, whose face showed nothing but contempt. It took Charlotte only a moment to choose a different face for herself. She placed a tender hand on Anne's forearm. "Anne... Annie," she said. "I've already forgiven you. It's over and done with...forgotten." She waited a second, but Anne was unable to respond through her tears. Charlotte comforted her sister more. "You've been under a terrible strain...enduring hard things, awful things. I remember how I felt when I found out I couldn't have more children after Little Annie was born. Stop crying. I'm not mad at you. You're my sister."

Anne leaned toward Charlotte and dissolved into full-out sobbing. Charlotte supported her sister's upper body as she spoke. "You have to relax about all this. You'll make yourself sick. You'll have a baby one day. Wait and see."

Anne spluttered out a few broken phrases to Charlotte. "I'm not crying about that. I'm crying from relief that you don't hate me."

Sallie leaned over to console Anne, as well. "Anne, Anne... Charlotte is family. Rose, too. They could never hate you. And as your mother, I'm choosing to believe it's God's will for you to have a baby, though in his own good time, not ours."

Rose stood up and looked down on the other three women, her eyes glassy with bitterness. "Don't buy what Anne is selling," she said to Charlotte as if Sallie, their mother, were not present. "The great Dr. York would still put you through carrying a baby for her if she thought she could get away with it, one kidney or no."

Rose shoved the plaque Anne had given her across the tabletop. "Give this piece of junk to somebody else. If Mom and Charlotte want to wallow around telling you how great you are, after what you did...that's for them, not me."

She gave Anne a last harsh look before stomping away from the terrace toward her children, who were still eating their popsicles on the grassy slope. Charlotte got up and followed Rose, catching her by her elbow. Rose shrugged her off and kept walking, stern-faced, stiff-necked, unwavering, unforgiving.

— *Anne* —

This is the juncture where I must admit yet another failing. After giving up on the clinic and turning my problems over to God, I began to view myself as a tragic heroine, which led to my acting the part. I became a somber character with a heartbreaking past (no baby). The reason for all this drama, much of which played out solely inside my own head, was this: I did not believe a hundred percent that God's will for my life would be better than my will. This lack of faith did not stop me from patting myself on my own back for deciding to pretend to put God first. I thought a great deal about how wonderful I had become, a modern-day martyr willing to be miserable for God, as if he needed or wanted my misery. My silly attitude resulted in much time wasted on soulful looks in the mirror, pitiful crying into my pillow on nights I gave into feeling sorry for myself (while Gabe lay beside me snoring peacefully), and lots of private thoughts that I would never have shared with anyone, all about how God must be viewing me as truly special in his eyes due to my new stoic attitude. I don't know if you are able to see this playacting in a comic light, but I can, on looking back...comic if it were not so ridiculous. I was enjoying my bogus righteousness. *Oh, oh, oh. See how good I am now for being humble before you, God, giving up my resentment over not being able to have a baby boy and accepting my painful lot in life (your terrible will for me) with such dignity.* What a sly and cunning personality self can be with its overt and covert ways of displaying pride. Only God knows the human heart, and only God can change it.

The heart is deceitful above all things, and desperately sick;
who can understand it?
I the Lord search the heart and examine the mind.
JEREMIAH 17:9-10A ESV

[Paul] *As the Scriptures say,*
"No one is righteous, not even one."
ROMANS 3:10 NLT

[Paul] *It is because of him (God) that you are in*
Christ Jesus, who has become for us wisdom from God,
that is, our righteousness, holiness, and redemption.
1 CORINTHIANS 1:30 NIV

Chapter

22

Gabe worked at gluing a tiny part onto his newly begun model ship. Anne came down the steps from the living area to the garage level carrying two mugs of hot tea. She set one on the worktable for Gabe and kept the other.

"Thanks," he said, pulling up a tall stool for his wife.

She glanced at her smartwatch as she settled onto the stool. "It's after midnight. What's the problem...can't sleep?"

Gabe shrugged. "Racing thoughts, brain out of control."

Anne steamed her nose in the mug for a moment before going on. "Me, too. I wish I could go back in time, undo things."

"Hey, it isn't your fault we're so far apart on...issues."

"That's why I came down here, to say you're right and I'm wrong...about everything."

Gabe wiped his hands on his pants and faced Anne. "Are you talking about the clinic? You sound different."

"Different is putting it mildly. I've been praying nonstop with no answers. And I'm finally seeing that God wants me to give up trying to force things. No discarding embryos, no selective reduction, no more injections, no more money down the drain." She breathed in deeply and exhaled with a cleansing sigh. "No IVF. In short, no more clinic."

"But you've never given up on a goal in your life. Why now?"

"Someone gave me a gift that got my attention."

"Who?"

Anne took a *New Testament* from her cardigan pocket and laid it gently on Gabe's worktable. "Jesus of Nazareth. He paid my sin debt on a cross." She watched with loving eyes as Gabe picked up the testament and gazed at its leather cover. Anne smiled. "Pastor Seabrook is a persistent dude," she said. "He has made a serious dent in my thick skull. Advised me to trust the Lord to take care of my needs, to humble myself before him and stop acting like I was doing him a favor in the process...if I ever wanted my prayers answered."

The hopeful look on Gabe's face melted away. "Oh, I get it. You still want a baby, only not by IVF. You're going to try prayer now." He put the testament back down and gave Anne a disappointed stare-down. Then, averting his sad eyes, he added, "I don't like the sound of it. Pastor Seabrook didn't mean you could start using God as a vending machine."

Dismayed, Anne said, "I deserve that, I guess. Rose would agree with you. You're both wrong, though. I've given up thinking I'm supposed to get my way all the time...prayed about it over and over with Pastor Seabrook. It's taken some repetition to get it to stick in my head that God wants to help me with everything, to the point of my turning all of it over to him, all the stuff my own selfishness would rather hang onto. Pastor Seabrook made me see that God's will for my life is better than anything I could ever dream up for myself. And I don't mean that in an egocentric sense. I mean it in a servant sense. It's why I'm trying to talk about it with you, Gabe, put it into words. I know how I've treated you. I wouldn't have blamed you if you had never come back. I wouldn't blame you if you left again."

Anne's tears began flowing at that point, making it difficult for her to squeak out what she had to say next. "But whether you leave or stay, I want you to know I care deeply about your model ships!" She punctuated the word, *ships*, with a little hiccup.

Gabe looked confused, then he chuckled. "My ships?" he said and chuckled again.

Anne wept more sloppily. "I couldn't figure out how else to put it," she cried. "I never cared about your old ships, or your job, or anything else important to you..." She wiped her leaky nose with the sleeve of her robe and wept louder. "So, I thought... Actually, Pastor Seabrook thought maybe you'd understand how serious I am about doing right by you if I told you I cared about your ships." More hiccuping.

Still laughing, Gabe wrapped his wife in his arms as she sobbed herself into an out of control crying jag. Gabe made funny faces and rolled his eyes as he comforted her. "Okay, fine...fine," he said. "Now that I know you care about my ships, everything is going to work out great. Pastor Seabrook is some kind of nutty genius."

— *Anne* —

What an amazing change, taking my first few awkward steps toward considering someone else's needs above my own? Gabe was right. It did take a genius like Pastor Seabrook to lead me down a better path, God's path. It is humiliating how I began my new journey. Gabe's model ships and wood art had been nowhere on my radar, his interests nothing to me, less than nothing. But after spending time with Pastor Seabrook, I began to see I was missing the point entirely. I ought to be loving my husband in an unselfish manner, and if that meant showing support for his hobbies, that's what I needed to do. Self was going to have to learn to take a back seat. I still feel terrible about being blind to Gabe's needs for so many years, though I'm not the only one with this deficiency. Even Peter the Apostle had moments of blindness. Would that I could become like Peter as he grew so mightily in service to others. Would that I could become like Jesus!

> *When they had finished breakfast, Jesus said to Simon Peter, "Simon, son of John, do you love me more than these?" He said to him, "Yes, Lord; you know that I love you." He said to him, "Feed my lambs." He said to him a second time, "Simon, son of John, do you love me?" He said to him, "Yes, Lord; you know that I love you." He said to him, "Tend my sheep." He said to him the third time, "Simon, son of John, do you love me?" Peter was grieved because he said to him the third time, "Do you love me?" and he said to him, "Lord, you know everything; you know that I love you." Jesus said to him "Feed my sheep."*
> JOHN 21:15-17 ESV

Even as the Son of Man [Jesus] came not to be served but to serve, and to give his life as a ransom for many.
MATTHEW 20:28B ESV

Chapter

23

Anne took three water skiing trophies and several photographs of her various graduations off the fireplace mantel and tossed them into a cardboard box. With great care, she lifted Gabe's biggest model ship from the floor, placed it on the mantel, and stood back to admire it.

When Gabe walked in, she was busy adjusting the model to line up perfectly with the center of the fireplace inset. He watched for a moment, confused, before noticing the cardboard box. Taking out one of the ski trophies, he held it up. "What about this?" he said. "University Women's Water skiing Championship - First Place."

"Maybe Rose would like to have it," Anne laughed, "for old time's sake. The only trophy she ever got was when her frog won the hopping contest at Vacation Bible School one summer." She pointed toward the model now occupying center stage on the mantel. "How does it look? There's room for two smaller pieces on either end. I'm kind of liking this new décor."

Gabe did not agree or disagree. "We need to talk," he said.

Anne scrunched her face. "Oh, no, not talk. Sounds ominous."

Gabe dropped the trophy back into the box with the

others, accidentally snapping off the plastic miniature skier. "All right, we'll call it a chat," he said, at the same time hefting the box and lumbering toward the exit that led down to the garage level. Anne followed Gabe, listening as he walked and talked. "We have to go to the bank..." he said, "...take out another personal loan."

Anne blinked in surprise. "What in the world for? I thought we'd given up all that debt nonsense."

"For the clinic...IVF."

"Isn't that going backward? We're supposed to be marching forward on faith along with God...baby or no baby. I meant it when I said I'm good either way."

⟪⟪⟪

Gabe entered the garage carrying the box full of Anne's trophies. She followed him foot to foot, confused by his new perspective. "I want a baby," he said, "in the worst way possible. It feels like some kind of emotional thing building up inside me that might explode any second. Do you think it's my biological time clock ticking?"

Anne, now unsure they were having a real conversation, said with a hint of her old smart-mouth. "I know a women's support group you can join. Meets once a week at Lucinda Maybank's office. Want me to sign you up?"

"No! I want us to do IVF. At least, I think I do. But before we decide for certain, I want to talk it over with Pastor Seabrook. Any guy who got it worked around to my favorite model ship occupying the living room mantel front and center...well, a guy that brilliant ought to be able to solve a simple little problem like infertility."

— *Anne* —

I decided to spare Gabe my negative mindset about the clinic. Bottom line? I did not want to go back there to be tortured, no matter if my fearful attitude hurt his feelings. I wanted to avoid the pain from the procedures themselves, not to mention the emotional upheaval I would be taking on. And not just for me...for Gabe, as well. How could I bear a repeat of getting our hopes up and then having to deal with the heartbreak of no baby if the procedures did not work? Why on earth, after God in his mercy had helped me make peace with my childlessness, would I want to start punishing myself - *ourselves!* - all over again? Moreover, I was weary of talking about it with Pastor Seabrook. He had been a lifesaver over those first weeks when I'd returned to praying and reading my *Bible.* Without his wise counsel, I may never have learned that submitting to God was the only way to real peace. And now here Gabe was telling me about a need of his own, one that sounded to my ears more like a want than a need, all of which threw me into confusion again. What more did God expect of me? Was it not enough I was giving money to Maria and her child; trying to be a better wife to Gabe; praying and reading my *Bible*; attending church again; spending more time helping Mom and my sisters take care of Dad? I was getting so used to engaging in those wholesome activities that I was almost to the point of enjoying them. And now here Gabe was asking me to stretch farther, do more, trust more, risk more. The last thing I wanted was to jump back into the path of heartbreak, not even for Gabe's sake...until I prayed about his newly expressed need and began to understand that my own role in God's plan for me was to help my husband, not deny him. God, it seemed, was giving me an excruciatingly difficult thing to do for the benefit of someone else, a sacrifice that self was not thrilled to make. Thank you, Father, for finally empowering me by your Holy Spirit to put self in its proper place...last!

> [Paul] *You, my brothers and sisters, were called to be free. But do not use your freedom to indulge the flesh; rather, serve one another humbly in love. For the entire law is fulfilled in keeping this one command:*
> *"Love your neighbor as yourself."*
> GALATIANS 5:13-14 NIV

> *When he (Jesus) had washed their feet and put on his outer garments and resumed his place, he said to them, "Do you understand what I have done to you? You call me Teacher and Lord, and you are right, for so I am. If I then, your Lord and Teacher, washed your feet, you also ought to wash one another's feet."*
> JOHN 13:12-14 ESV

Chapter

24

Anne and Gabe sat opposite Pastor Seabrook's desk. The aging minister frowned, lining his already craggy face deeper. "Why are you asking me? I'm a preacher, not a prophet," he said. "I've got problems of my own."

Anne and Gabe glanced at each other. Gabe ventured a tentative response. "Uh...we thought since you're clergy, you'd be able to help us figure out what to do next. Should we go back to the clinic? Try more procedures? Not try at all? We don't know."

"That makes three of us." The gray-haired minister snapped the pencil with which he was fiddling. "Did I hear you say you're together on the discarding thing? And selective reduction?" He picked up a second pencil and snapped it.

Anne tried to clarify. "No," she said. "I mean, yes, we're together. Not doing either one. We've sort of begun questioning everything associated with in vitro. What's your take on it?"

The preacher found a third pencil to break. "I don't know enough about it to have a take. Except for some parts, which are dead wrong, the ones you've already taken off the table. The rest is beyond my experience." He started to snap the third pencil, but instead dropped it to his desktop on realizing his behavior was getting weird. He picked up his reading glasses and turned them over and over in his hands, thinking...wondering aloud, "Maybe if we try to put it in some other context. Say if you had cancer, you'd go to an oncologist; or an ulcer, an internist; cataracts, an ophthalmologist; a broken bone, an orthopedist. Stands to reason then..."

Gabe interrupted him. "Stands to reason you're afraid to express an opinion. You aren't going to snap your glasses in two, are you?"

The preacher bristled and laid the glasses down on a legal pad with a bit too heavy a hand. He grabbed his last good pencil and snapped it hard. "You make me sound like a coward when you say it like that...afraid to express an opinion. If I had an opinion, I'd express it. I just don't happen to have one. Trying to think how I'd feel if a loved one of mine were suffering from infertility. The one thing I know for sure, the kinds of clinics we're talking about have helped thousands of desperate couples. Who am I to say every procedure they offer is wrong? Nope, can't say that. Don't know enough."

Anne jumped in, frustrated. "But you're a preacher. You must know something."

The exasperated Pastor Seabrook picked up his glasses again and put them on. He peered over them at Anne. "Did you not hear me? I don't know a thing. All I can do is pray for God's guidance."

"Wait," Anne said, interrupting him a second time. "Let's think it through logically. If it's my egg, Gabe's sperm, and one embryo at a time, how can it be wrong?"

"For the two of you, it probably isn't," said Pastor Seabrook, "although I wish to high Heaven I did not have to hear about anyone's eggs and sperm. But for all couples in all circumstances, I can't say if it's right or wrong. Maybe it's like in the *Bible,* eating meat offered to idols is questionable only if it sets a poor example and leads people astray."

It was Anne's turn to furrow her brow. "Eating what?"

"Never mind," said the pastor. "Let's pray."

Gabe and Anne exchanged uneasy looks again before bowing their heads with Pastor Seabrook, who let out a heavy sigh as he tried to prepare himself for entering the presence of Holy God. After enough time had passed to make his counselees even more uncomfortable, the good pastor began mumbling under his breath. "Oh, Lord God Almighty, if you're listening to me, if you hear me, I have something to tell you that's honest and true. I have no idea what to pray for these two young people sitting here before me, so I'm asking you to pray for them, Lord. May your Holy Spirit speak on their behalf with discernment and power. Thank you, Father, in the name of Jesus. Amen."

— *Anne* —

Pastor Seabrook's jumpiness opened my eyes to something I had not grasped before, that Gabe and I were not alone as we stumbled along the bumpy road of infertility. Our loving pastor had joined us, and not only that, he'd brought along his own anxiety. His agitation in that last counseling session made it clear he did not have all the answers, which was not sitting well with the conscientious servant of God. Nevertheless, his position as our shepherd had cast him in the starring role of having to do his best to try to help us. It was interesting and wise on his part to involve the Holy Spirit in prayer instead of trying to drive things himself. Spiritual wisdom guided by the mind of Christ was what Gabe and I needed, which was the kind of supernatural wisdom Pastor Seabrook insisted on seeking. It is odd how much I learned from him that morning by not learning much at all. He demonstrated in practical terms that when you don't know how to solve a difficult problem, you need to lay it down at the foot of the cross and leave it there. And Pastor Seabrook, in utter humility, helped Gabe and me do exactly that. Thank you, Jesus, for giving our beloved shepherd the good sense to acknowledge his limitations. He sought to put us in the center of God's will by placing us in the hands of the all-knowing Holy Spirit. Thank you, Spirit, for hearing this good man's prayer for us. And thank you more for teaching us how to listen for your response. Amen.

> [Jesus] *If you love me, obey my commandments. And I will ask the Father, and he will give you another Advocate, who will never leave you. He is the Holy Spirit, who leads you into all truth. The world cannot receive him, because it isn't*

looking for him and doesn't recognize him. But you know him, because he lives with you now, and later will be in you. I will not abandon you as orphans. I will come to you.
JOHN 14:15-18 NLT

[Jesus] *But when the Father sends the Advocate as my representative - that is, the Holy Spirit - he will teach you everything and will remind you of everything I have told you.*
JOHN 14:26 NLT

[Jesus to his disciples before he ascended to Heaven] *I have much more to say to you, more than you can bear now. But when he, the Spirit of truth, comes, he will guide you into all the truth. He will not speak on his own; he will speak only what he hears, and he will tell you what is yet to come. He will glorify me because it is from me that he will receive what he will make known to you. All that belongs to the Father is mine. That is why I said the Spirit will receive from me what he will make known to you.*
JOHN 16:12-15 NIV

Chapter

25

Gabe spoke first as he and Anne walked together down the hall outside Pastor Seabrook's study. "That was helpful...*not*," he said with disgust.

Anne echoed his annoyed tone. "I thought preachers knew more."

Gabe slowed their pace to ponder the situation. "At least, he didn't judge us like a lot of guys in his position would've done. Never mind the planks in their own eyes."

"Planks?"

Gabe's patience with the entire day had worn thin. He could take no more of Anne's nonsense. "Oh, for crying out loud. You don't know about eating meat offered to idols – not because it's wrong, but could lead someone else astray, all symbolic, of course – and you don't know you're not supposed to judge a person for having a speck in his eye when you've got a plank in your own, again symbolic." He paused a beat. "You don't seem to know anything worthwhile?"

"I can't believe you're judging my ignorance about the *Bible*, and me in a highly emotional state from being infertile."

"The *Bible* also says not to be touchy."

Anne sniffed. "Well then, stop being touchy, why don't you?" she said. "I think Pastor Seabrook was trying to tell us that if we're sick,we ought to see a doctor. Remember he was talking about how if you had cancer, you'd go to an oncologist, and all those other hypothetical medical conditions and specialists? Sounded like he was implying, in a wimpy kind of way without coming right out and saying it, that if you're in sick mode with infertility, maybe you should see an infertility specialist. And in our case, the specialist happens to be at the clinic."

"Maybe. He didn't mind nixing selective reduction and discarding embryos. That was clear enough. He must figure a lot of the other stuff that he doesn't know about is between us and God. Let's face it. Our pastor has bowed out."

Anne paused. "Guess that's better than handing out worthless advice." She waited a second before adding, "Are you getting any vibes from God?"

"Yeah, jackhammer vibes, all of which are telling me that IVF would be okay for us, but with one egg and a single embryo transfer from petri dish to womb."

Anne nodded assent, though her countenance was thoughtful, not joyful. "Which means you were right about calling the bank. Those loan officers will jump at the chance to lend us more dough for the sole reason that I'm a doctor. Kind of dumb on their part."

"Doesn't matter how dumb they are as long as they cough up the money. We're stepping out on faith here, Annie. And if the result is no baby, we'll accept that as God's will and go forward praising and thanking him, maybe even asking him about adoption."

"Okay," Anne said, "to the bank, we go, and then to the clinic."

Gabe gave her a fist bump. "On faith seeking God's will"

Anne stopped in her tracks, her expression troubled. "Uhm...I've done something you need to know about."

Gabe stopped walking, too, and gripped her hand, forcing her to make eye contact. "What now?"

"Well," Anne began with hesitation. "While Pastor Seabrook was praying for us back there in his office, I restated silently a selfish vow I made to God a while back, on the night I went to the church sanctuary and lit all those candles."

"Vow?" Gabe said, not sounding thrilled.

Anne pulled her wrist out of his grasp and rubbed it. "But this time it was more like a bargain...that if God would give us a son, we'd raise him as a consecrated boy."

Gabe frowned and kneaded his forehead. "You can't negotiate with God, Anne. We don't even have to run that one by Pastor Seabrook. I already know."

"I do, too...now. But I didn't back then. It's why I amended my promise today in Pastor Seabrook's office, while he was praying aloud. I told God in my mind that if he were willing to give us a baby boy, I'd honor my earlier promise, the one I made when I thought I could negotiate, but this time I'd honor it out of praise and gratitude, love, and obedience, not some stupid idea I could pay back a blessing. Who did I think I was when I tried that on, some puny lesser god?"

"Okay, so not a vow of negotiation, just a promise of

gratitude with legs on it, no matter what God has in mind for you? The question is...will you still be grateful if you don't get what you want?"

"Yes, but that doesn't mean I can't pray about what's in my heart. The main thing I need from God right now is help with putting his will above mine, and somehow wanting to. It's odd, but at this moment, he's giving me peace, and not only peace, but joy and gratitude no matter what comes my way. Guess he's providing those blessings, too."

"All right then, to the bank, doll face. Praise Jesus for one more debt!"

Anne hugged Gabe and cried a bit, though smiling at the same time. "And praise him that we can pay it off whenever the house sells."

— *Anne* —

My resolve remained firm as Gabe and I walked into the clinic in our new obedience. And yet, I could not help wondering with human trepidation how many times God was going to allow me to be tormented by infertility. I also wondered if perhaps my and Gabe's current involvement with the clinic had to do with infertility at all. Maybe it was God's way of showing me that serving others – Gabe, in this instance – was my most important calling. Could it be that situations and contexts were not always about me? Don't laugh. I cannot be the only woman who has lived for decades thinking the same thing. I assure you, as I stepped foot back into the clinic with Gabe, it felt like the beginning of a special torture session custom-designed just for me. And the strange thing was that Gabe never realized I was doing it for him. Well, mostly for him. I still held onto a shred of hope of my own, though what I did *not* want was more disappointment. By this time, I was beginning to understand that God was giving me a gift I may never have received if I had not suffered the plight of infertility. He was showing me that he alone could change my heart. Not to say I didn't know it needed changing. (Thank you, Rose, for pointing this out to me so willingly, if coldly.) Though what to do next was still a mystery. It was only after I had left Rose's house on the day I went there to apologize, and stopped on my way home to pray alone, that I realized I had lost my way again. I thought I was supposed to be asking for God's help as I tried to change my heart by personal will alone. It took me a while to figure out God was changing it for me, healing me, causing me to desire to do good and be good for his sake, not mine. I am here today to declare to you in certain terms I could never have achieved such a thing by my lonesome. It was a gift from our generous Heavenly Father, a gift I did not deserve any more than any of us deserve salvation by God's grace through the sacrifice of his Son on the cross. I know now that every good thing is a gift from God...every single good thing! He even gives us the faith and trust we need to relax and enjoy his perfect will for our lives, for he is faithful like that. Thank you, God, for sharing your holy goodness with me.

Every good and perfect gift is from above,
coming down from the Father of the heavenly lights,
in whom there is no change or shifting shadow.
JAMES 1:17 BSB

He restoreth my soul:
He leadeth me in the paths of righteousness
for his name's sake.
PSALM 23:3 KJV

Trust in the Lord with all your heart and
lean not on your own understanding;
in all your ways submit to him,
and he will make your paths straight.
PROVERBS 3:5-6 NIV

Chapter

26

Dr. Armond's face went from serene to disturbed as Gabe outlined his and Anne's firm parameters concerning IVF. The seasoned doctor leaned forward in his desk chair and stared at Anne for agreement with Gabe's explanation, or preferably disagreement. Said he with a mocking tone, "A single egg from you and one collection of sperm cells from Mr. Simmons? Is that honestly what you're proposing?"

Anne nodded. Dr. Armond leaned back again in his chair and took in both Anne and Gabe's faces with a cold stare. "What you're describing is in no way protocol here," he said. "You need better odds than that considering the amount of money it will cost, not to mention the physical discomfort you'll be in for, Dr. York. The lead-up injections, pain and cramping, egg retrieval, for a single shot at getting pregnant. I cannot supervise an IVF attempt with those limitations. They are too stringent. I can't, not in good conscience."

Gabe had no trouble standing up to Dr. Armond's arrogance. "You don't understand, sir. What we're saying is that we can't - *we won't* - do IVF any other way...not in good conscience."

Dr. Armond looked down his nose at Gabe. "And what you don't understand, Mr. Simmons, is that it would be a guarantee for failure. I cannot take your money under such circumstances."

"Sure, you can take our money. We know the odds are stacked against us. But that's not what we're talking about now, is it? We're talking about whether or not you'll take our money."

"You don't know what you're asking," said the doctor.

"Oh, we know all right...you want our money."

"I don't like your tone, sir."

"You're right, Dr. Armond, and I'm sorry for being so forthright. But you said it yourself. People suffering from infertility get out of whack sometimes."

"I meant women, not men."

Gabe ignored the jab. "We need you, doctor...your skills and expertise. This is it for us, our last try. We want to give it our best shot with the best doctor...*you.*"

"No other reputable clinic would try IVF this way."

"Oh, yes, they would...for money."

"I said reputable."

Dr. Armond picked up the receiver of his desk phone. "Melissa," he said, "would you be so kind as to assist Dr. York and Mr. Simmons with scheduling appointments leading up to IVF. They are leaving my office now. Meet them in the hallway, please, and show them to yours. Thanks."

He hung up the phone and refocused on Anne and Gabe, then he shrugged as if washing his hands of certain failure. "As long as you both know it won't work," he said.

Gabe did not blink as he returned the man's steady gaze.

"We're doing it this way out of faith in God, Dr. Armond, and obedience, the best we can discern as obedience, anyway. And if no baby comes of it, we'll know we tried in the only way right for us. That's enough...more than enough."

— Anne —

Don't tell anyone, but I secretly wished Dr. Armond had been successful in talking Gabe out of IVF. Then I could have said to God, "*Look at me, Lord, how unselfishly I'm treating my husband. See what hard things I was willing to put myself through on his behalf. Too bad Dr. Armond stopped me, which was not my fault. I still deserve credit, though, for being willing to make sacrifices for Gabe, even though I didn't want to.*" Self was doing a great deal of that kind of thinking in the recesses of my mind. And though I never verbalized those self-interested musings, I did harbor them in private, and a lot. It occurred to me more than once that if Dr. Armond had not let Gabe talk him into trying an unusual IVF procedure with us as a couple, I may have been able to get credit on God's economic balance sheet for attempting to do a difficult good deed that I did not even have to complete. Everybody knows that feeling. It's like when you invite people over for an elaborate dinner, and they say they can't make it because of their schedules, and you think inside your guilty mind that you are glad they can't, but you are also glad you got credit for inviting them. Don't tell me you haven't ever felt that way. But this time it was not meant to be. No getting credit for a good deed without having to actually do it. Once again, I found myself on the road to IVF, the road I was so desperate to travel a few short weeks ago, but now did not want to travel at all. The only way I could make myself take those first few steps forward was to repeat over and over inside my mind, I'm doing this for Gabe in obedience to God. I did not want to go through with it, and yet God through his grace and empowerment gave me faith, trust, and strength to endure. By grace, I mean God's willingness to provide his help and gifts that we do not deserve. Interestingly, my undeserving condition was the one thing I had come to understand in full. I did not understand much else, but I knew myself to be unworthy and in need of grace. Thank you, Father, for your mercy on me! Amen.

For by grace you have been saved through faith.
And this is not your own doing; it is the gift of God,
not a result of work, so that no one may boast.
EPHESIANS 2:8-9 ESV

There is therefore now no condemnation
for those who are in Christ Jesus.
ROMANS 8:1 ESV

In him we have redemption through his blood,
the forgiveness for sins, in accordance with the riches
of God's grace that he lavished on us.
EPHESIANS 1:7-8A NIV

Chapter

Anne's vibrating phone in the pocket of her lab coat broke her concentration. Irritated at being interrupted from listening to her pregnant patient's belly with her stethoscope, she jerked the phone out of her pocket and saw that the fertility clinic was calling. It took only a click to decline the call so that she could focus again on her patient.

"Everything is going great, Darla," Anne said. "Your baby is growing like a weed. You can get dressed now. See you next month."

Again, the phone began vibrating, this time in Anne's hand as she exited the exam room. She answered it in the hallway on her way to her office. "Dr. York here," she said on entering her private space and closing the door. A clinic nurse on the other end of the line acknowledged her. Anne heard the sympathetic woman out before responding with sadness. "Negative?" she said. "Not pregnant? Any point in testing again?" She held her breath while the nurse delivered the second half of the awful message. Anne worked at keeping her voice under control as she ended the conversation. "All right, thank you," she said to the nurse. "It's okay. I'm okay. None of this is your fault. We expected it. Goodbye."

She touched the OFF button on her phone and leaned

back on the inside of her office door. Squeezing her eyes shut to fight the pain, she fought tears that came anyway. It took every ounce of her concentration to keep from throwing herself on the floor. With clenched jaw, she began praying feverishly, fervently. "Okay, God. I get it...no baby." She took a moment to settle herself before going on. "It just hurts so bad, but even with that, I'm choosing to trust you, trust your will for Gabe and me. You've given me faith, Savior Jesus, for which I'm grateful. I know I'm supposed to thank you for this adversity...count it all for joy as Mom would say. But I'm not there yet, Lord. I can't do it fully. I'll keep on praying, though, until I can." She lost control and began weeping, her chest heaving. "Thank you, God," she said, grimacing and weeping as she spoke. "Thank you for this adversity that I do not understand."

Anne forced herself back to composure. Then she walked with resolve to her desk, took off her lab coat, tossed it across the back of the desk chair, opened the side drawer and jerked out her purse, rummaged through it until she found the keys to her old Ford, slung the purse strap over her shoulder, and walked in purposeful strides back toward her office door.

Once in the hallway again, she picked up her pace to try to rush by the receptionist's desk without being accosted. Which did not work. Carmen, Anne's receptionist, called out to her in anxious tones. "Dr. York? Dr. York, are you leaving for the day? Michelle Wilson is on the line. She says it's an emergency, wants to talk to you, not a nurse."

Though irritated at being caught, Anne stopped and dealt with the problem professionally. "Is she in labor? Does she think she's in labor?"

"No, just really bad constipated."

"Tell her she's supposed to call her grandma about things like that. And to stop eating so much cheese and stick with oatmeal! Call me if she goes into labor, or if anyone else does."

Anne exited before Carmen could set up more chatter. The last she saw of her receptionist, she was still on the phone, one hand covering the receiver, her face pale and distressed. Anne muttered to herself as she made her escape down the front walkway. "Eight-and-a-half-months pregnant and constipated. Nobody could count that for joy."

— *Anne* —

You can see why I had been reluctant to go back to the clinic. My Heavenly Father had been merciful to me. He'd given me peace in my heart about having no baby, and then, out of nowhere, Gabe had begun troubling the waters again. What woman would not feel frustrated at having to consider her husband's needs over her own about something as important as that? I thought it was too much for God to expect of me, and yet expect it of me, he did. I obeyed, though not out of utter submission, not quite. I got it into my head that if I yielded and put Gabe's needs first, God might reward me. To be clear, I was not yielding because I wanted to please him or love him or even love Gabe. I was yielding because I hoped for supernatural favor in return for my sacrifice, favor I did not receive. What I got was yet another opportunity to be thankful for *not* being blessed with what I wanted. When the clinic nurse told me I wasn't pregnant, I felt like I was drowning. I had gotten my hopes up, despite trying not to, and the bad news was a terrible blow. I had read in the *Bible* that the Holy Spirit would never leave me alone in painful situations. I tried to remember this, even as I hung onto a measure of resentment that the IVF attempt had not even been my idea. I had gone along with it out of what I saw as a valiant effort to meet Gabe's needs, and now I was sinking in pain again. I felt solitary as I prayed for strength to be thankful, and yet I knew I was not alone. I was in the company of the greatest Comforter of all, God's Holy Spirit.

> And I [Jesus] *will pray the Father, and he shall give you*
> *another Comforter, that he may abide with you forever;*
> *Even the Spirit of truth; whom the world cannot receive,*

because it seeth him not, neither knoweth him: but ye know him; for he dwelleth with you and shall be in you.

JOHN 14:16-17 KJV

Chapter

28

Anne entered the church sanctuary from the vestibule doors. She had driven straight there from her office after receiving the worst possible news from the clinic. She paused a moment, looking around at the beauty of the space. Then she walked down the center aisle, dropped her purse on the altar steps, approached the altar, and knelt. Prayer had become her solace of late, and solace was what she needed at this heartrending moment.

Pastor Seabrook shuffled in unexpectedly and spied her there. He cleared his throat to alert her to his presence. She got to her feet and moped over to where he was standing. He spoke to her in a soothing voice. "Is everything all right? Last time I saw you in here alone..."

Anne blessed him with a smile, sickly though it was. She looked tired. Even her voice sounded weary. "I didn't bring candles this time. No fire hazard. I'm here thanking God for adversities...trying to, anyway. Haven't quite got the hang of it yet...still rote words, but I'm not giving up."

Pastor Seabrook reached out and touched her arm. "Did something happen? Is your dad all right?"

"Just got a call from the clinic...we're not going to be having a baby." She choked back tears for the second time that morning. "I came over to thank God for the bad news, to officially reaffirm my trust and faith that his plan for me is best, not my selfish wants. And I also needed to pull myself together before calling Gabe. This is going to be rough on him." She paused a moment, dreading the call. "He'll be disappointed."

Pastor Seabrook took a folded paper out of his hip pocket and stared at it a second before handing it to Anne. She unfolded it and cringed on realizing what it was. Pastor Seabrook spoke up quickly to ease her embarrassment. "I've been carrying that around a while. You left it on the altar steps the night of your candlelight vigil. Anyway, I kept it. Don't know why."

Anne's face went crimson. She tore the paper in half, then quarters, eighths, and sixteenths and handed the pieces back to her old friend. She spoke through clenched teeth. "I was trying to negotiate with God. Arrogant, huh."

"I thought it was kind of sweet," said the pastor, "promising the Lord to bring up a son consecrated. I'm sorry, but I read what you wrote...couldn't stop myself."

"Sweet for Hannah in the *Old Testament,* maybe, but not for me. It was one more conniving effort to grab what I wanted when I wanted it. I've been trying to get rid of that cockeyed attitude...even prayed to God I'd keep my vow if he would make it his will to give me a son." She touched the torn pieces of paper in Pastor Seabrook's hands. "But the second time, I promised to keep it out of gratitude and praise, not debt service. I've done a lot of thinking about Hannah, Samuel's mother. Seems to me her vow was a promise of gratitude, too, not negotiation. Just plain old thankfulness. I love that she calmed right down after Ely, the priest, prayed for her. It was like she had come to accept whatever God had in store for her. I don't know...maybe I'm reading too much into it now that my own faith has come back. The phone call from the clinic showed me it really is possible to feel gratitude for something counterintuitive, like no baby. God denied me the most important desire of my life, something I thought I could not live without, and somehow, I'm at peace with it...almost."

"Counterintuitive...at peace though your heart is breaking," said Pastor Seabrook.

"Right now, it doesn't feel like it's breaking. It did initially, when the call first came, but the pain of it started easing off as soon as I started praying." She looked at the floor as if something worrisome had come back to mind. "I have to call Gabe now," she said in a whisper. "Will you stay with me?"

Anne pulled her cell phone out of her pocket. It began vibrating in her hand, which startled her out of her gloom. She stared at the phone's small screen. "It's the clinic again," she said, "the last place I want to hear from."

She grimaced and touched the green button. "Dr. York here."

The clinic nurse on the other end of the line sounded upset. "Oh, Dr. York. I'm so relieved you answered. There's been a mistake. A tech got your test results mixed up with another patient's. Yours is positive, not negative. You're pregnant. I'm so sorry we got it wrong."

Anne listened to the nurse's news without blinking. Pastor Seabrook stood by, waiting, wondering. Anne remained frozen in body and voice, unable to do anything but stare straight ahead.

The clinic nurse went on chattering. Her words filled the silence left by Anne's inability to speak. "Dr. York? Are you still there? It's not a mistake this time. We've checked and rechecked a dozen times."

Anne searched for words. "But..." she began haltingly, "...this means the other woman isn't pregnant? Have you told her yet? What terrible news it'll be."

"No, no. We never called her in the first place. She won't get anything but the non-pregnant results...awful enough. Poor thing will never know we made the mistake, unless someone tells."

"Oh, I'm so sorry for her" Anne said. "It's heartbreaking, excruciating. But are you absolutely sure about me?"

"Everybody in the clinic is sure. Half the town is sure. Dr. Armond has been on the warpath the last hour."

"Thank you. Thanks so much. I need to call my husband. Thank you."

"Congratulations, Dr. York, and I appreciate your not being angry. Bye now."

Anne clicked off her phone and tried to assimilate the information. She began laughing and crying at the same time. Pastor Seabrook laughed with her, but he left off the bawling. "Was that what I think?" he said.

Anne shoved her phone back into her pocket, grabbed the pastor's hands, clamped her eyes shut, and prayed aloud. "Oh, dear God, thank you for mercy and favor. Amen."

She opened her eyes and bear-hugged her old counselor. "Someone made a mistake at the clinic," she said, smiling.

"Now the nurse is telling me I'm pregnant, and she's sure. Praise Jesus, she's sure!"

She hugged Pastor Seabrook again, so hard this time that he yelped. Then she hurried to snatch her purse from the altar steps and run up the aisle toward the vestibule doors, stopping midway to run back to the altar. Dropping to her knees, she prayed in a loud voice. "Oh, thank you, thank you, God, for adversities...I mean blessings! Thank you, Holy Spirit, for favor! Thank you, Jesus! Amen!"

She scrambled to her feet again and raced back up the aisle toward the front exit, brushing past the smiling Pastor Seabrook in a whoosh. In happy hysterics, she yelled back to him. "I'll call you later about scheduling the baby's dedication service. We have to make sure we get on your calendar. It's only eight months away, you know."

She flung open the vestibule doors and flew through to the outside. Pastor Seabrook shouted toward the empty doorway. "Aren't you going to call Gabe?"

"I want to tell him in person," she shouted back as the ornate doors swung shut behind her. Pastor Seabrook slapped his knee and laughed aloud. "Thank you, sweet Jesus, for mercy!" he said with unfiltered joy. Then he tossed the pieces of Anne's torn-up vow into the air and let them flutter about his upturned face.

— *Anne* —

Urgency filled my heart in those first few hours as news that I was pregnant became real to me. I felt desperate to get word to Gabe as soon as possible, fearful the reality of the blessing might vanish before I could let him know. Random Scripture passages flowed through my mind like streams in a desert as I rushed about trying to find him, the most poignant being *Psalm 30:5b ESV Weeping may tarry for the night, but joy comes with the morning.* Yet, the joy of my new blessing was not the only experience that visited me in those early hours. A realization I did not expect entered my heart. It was as if it sought and found a particular empty space that had been waiting for it all along. I understood with a jolt that I had been catapulted into the category Jesus described in *Luke 12:48b NLT When someone has been given much, much will be required in return; and when someone has been entrusted with much, even more will be required.* I saw instantly that bringing up our son as a consecrated boy out of gratitude to God was not going to be enough. (Of course, the baby was a boy!) There was something else God wanted me to do. And though at first my mind was too euphoric to process what that something was (starting prayer-based support groups for women suffering from infertility), I knew the details would come to me in God's will and timing. I did not fret. I just enjoyed being pregnant and hurried to share the news with Gabe so that he could enjoy it with me. He and I had made the hard decision to rejoice in the Lord in sadness. Now we would rejoice in gladness. Thank you, Jesus, for being with us in both. We are grateful! Amen.

*Though the fig tree does not bud and there are no grapes on
the vines, though the olive crop fails and the fields produce
no food, though there are no sheep in the pen and no cattle
in the stalls, yet I will rejoice in the Lord. I will be joyful in
God my Savior. The Sovereign Lord is my strength;
he makes my feet like the feet of a deer,
he enables me to tread on the heights.*

HABAKKUK 3:17-19A NIV

*God's way is perfect. All the Lord's promises prove true.
He is a shield for all who look to him for protection.
For who is God except the Lord?
Who but our God is a solid rock?
God arms me with strength, and he makes my way perfect.
He makes me as surefooted as a deer,
enabling me to stand on mountain heights.*

PSALM 18:30-33 NLT

Chapter

Anne flew into her kitchen like a wild bird. A brief search turned up Gabe's cell phone on the cluttered counter top. She slid the phone to the side of the yellow legal pad on which it lay. Gabe had scribbled a note-to-self that was barely legible on the pad. Anne deciphered it aloud, *"Fix Manuel's truck tomorrow morning."* She closed her eyes and thought hard. "Tomorrow," she whispered. "He wrote this last night, so tomorrow is today."

She bolted out of the kitchen, raced toward the foyer, and ran out the front door without locking it behind her. Within seconds she was clamoring into the driver's seat of her Ford relic, starting the engine (which took three heroic tries), and backing out of the driveway with a screech of bald tires. The old Ford backfired and shot out a puff of gray smoke from its muffler as Anne wheeled it like a race car around the sharp curve out of the neighborhood, which drew critical attention from the ever-present joggers on patrol. Though Anne didn't care what anyone saw or heard, not even when a rusty section of her back bumper fell off and landed with a clank on the asphalt. She ignored the sweaty crime watchers and drove faster.

Gabe and Manuel worked under the hood of Manuel's truck as several other men at the opposite end of the driveway tinkered with a collection of lawn mowers and weed trimmers. Manuel's sister, Maria, took time out from tending her small son to pour lemonade into plastic cups for the working men.

Anne drove into the driveway in the rusty Ford, crunching gravel as she scraped to a stop. Her eyes darted here and there as she scoped the area, soon spying Gabe's backside protruding from under the hood of Manuel's truck. She tapped on the horn before sliding out of the vehicle to hurry over to Gabe and Manuel, smiling and waving as she approached.

The distressed Maria grabbed up her child and hid behind a tree. She peeped from around it at Anne. The pretty Latina hugged her child close to her chest as she watched Anne talk to Gabe with excited gesturing. Gabe grinned, dropped his tools, hugged Anne, picked her up, swung her around. Manuel shouted the good news about the baby in Spanish to everyone in the vicinity.

They all smiled, clapped, and cheered, except for Maria, who crossed herself and looked up at the sky. Holding her child close, she waved her free hand upward toward Heaven as if thanking God that Anne was pregnant. Maria patted her little boy's back and kissed him and laughed as she watched Anne and Gabe embrace. Only then did she emerge with her child from their hiding place and walk in the direction of the happy couple, smiling and nodding happiness toward them when they noticed her.

Anne wriggled out of Gabe's arms and stepped toward Maria. She embraced the girl and the toddler as if they were family. The men nearby had grouped up on the lawn, grinning and slapping each other on the back as if they were the ones who had accomplished something. Everyone in Manuel's family showered their guests with happy Spanish, not a word of which Gabe or Anne understood.

⸙

Rose and Charlotte busied themselves pouring potting soil from large bags into several flowerpots. The terra cotta pots looked cheerful perched along the narrow surface of the low terrace wall. As the two sisters worked, their daughters played on the lawn with Frisbees and a water hose. Grandmother Sallie paid them no mind. Her attention was on Nick, her sick husband, making sure he ate everything on his lunch tray. She did not notice at first when Anne and Gabe walked around the side of the house, smiling and waving, calling out. Anne shouted to her parents in her brightest voice, one that had been dull far too long. "Hi, Mom, Dad. Wow! We all showed up today!"

Sallie broke into a huge smile. "Oh, my goodness. Look Nick. Anne and Gabe are here."

Nick grinned and held up his tea glass in welcome. "More, the merrier," he said. "Pull up a chair and have some of this delicious strained spinach Sallie is shoving down my throat."

Charlotte and Rose looked up from their work. Rose's face went sour. She watched with loathing as Anne and Gabe hugged Nick and Sallie and joined them in chairs at the umbrella table.

Not that Rose's attitude had any effect. Nothing could have spoiled Anne's mood. She could not stop smiling at her parents. "We came to bring y'all some good news," she gushed. "You tell them, Gabe."

"Nothing much," said the glowing father-to-be, "just that you're going to be grandparents again." He leaned over and patted Anne's belly.

Sallie lifted both hands high in the air. "Oh, happy day, happy day!" she yelled. Then she grabbed Anne by her shoulders and squeezed her, motioning Gabe to lean closer so that she could hug him at the same time. Still clinging to Anne and Gabe and laughing, she called out to Charlotte and Rose. "Did you hear, girls? Another baby in the family. We're thrilled, Anne, Gabe...thrilled."

Nick gained enough color in his face to make him look almost well. He beat Gabe on his back and then shook his hand, smiling and smiling more. Charlotte took off her garden gloves and walked across the terrace toward Anne, grinning as broadly as her father. "I'm overjoyed for you, Annie. You, too, Gabe. So happy. Really."

Rose kept her garden gloves on and stayed with the flowerpots. "Congratulations, Anne," she said from far away. "What a wonderful new accomplishment. You, too, Gabe. Congrats."

Anne rose and crossed the distance to Rose, trying to make eye contact as she walked. "I'm asking for your help, Rosie. I can't do this without you."

Rose harumphed. "Sure, you can. You can do anything. Ask Daddy."

"Not this. Please say you'll be there for me...and the baby. I need you. I've always needed you."

"I'll be there with bells on for whatever, same as always for everybody else in the family. Loyal dependable Rose." She stared into Anne's eyes for a defiant moment, then dropped her cold gaze and went back to filling the flowerpots.

Anne started to touch Rose's shoulder from behind, but stopped herself before making contact. She glanced at Sallie still at the table with Nick and Gabe, who mouthed *no* to her. Anne placed her hand on her own chest and stared with longing at the back of Rose's head.

— Anne —

I was twenty-four weeks pregnant and big in the belly by the time we sold the monster house with the monster mortgage. Unlike Gabe and me, the new owners could afford a mansion on a hill. And when we found a smaller house that suited our budget, we made sure we could make the payments out of my income alone, our goal since we realized Gabe's lack of a job was a blessing instead of a curse. He was elated when I told him about the modern concept of stay-at-home dads. He did a happy dance, literally, in the middle of our downsized living room. We solved the problem of the massive pieces of furniture in the mansion by including everything in the final sales contract. Furnishings for our new abode consisted of odds and ends from Mama and Daddy's attic, plus a few purchases from local junk shops. Our one splurge was the nursery. We shopped online for that important little haven. After everything we had gone through to become parents, Gabe insisted we deserved the pleasure of going a little overboard on making our baby's room special. My favorite spot in the nursery was the chair designed for nursing moms. I spent many an hour in that comfortable glider with my feet propped on its matching ottoman, baby-care books in hand, enjoying Gabe's presence as he assembled furniture and worked on the nursery wall mural. It was a lovely time in our lives, marred only by Daddy's deteriorating condition. It became clearer by the day that he might not live to see our baby. It was hard on an overachiever like me not being able to hurry things along for his sake. But in this case, I could do nothing but lean on God and accept his will, the recurring lesson and theme of my new life. Still, though, I prayed for Daddy to live for a few more months.

*Do not be anxious about anything, but in every situation,
by prayer and petition, with thanksgiving,
present your requests to God.*
PHILIPPIANS 4:6 NIV

Chapter

30

Anne floated through life in a weightless state for a month after she found out she was pregnant. Shock? Surprise? Pregnancy brain? Or simple mental and emotional confusion at having to adjust to a different reality?

It was not until after the rosy haze burned away that she recalled the troubling word of caution Pastor Seabrook had offered prior to her round of apologies. "You're aware, of course," he had said, "that one or two folks you've hurt might not buy into your dramatic I'm-so-sorries. It could take years for some people to forgive you, if ever."

Which, Anne knew, accounted for Rose's prolonged cold shoulder. She also knew she deserved being shut out by Rose, but it vexed her all the same. The sad thing was that several weeks into it, Anne's initial hurt at being snubbed by Rose began to morph into prickly resentment, a reaction Gabe called out as ridiculous.

"Let me get this straight," he said when Anne goaded him into talking about it, an activity he considered a waste of time. "You think Rose owes you an apology for not accepting your lame apology to her?"

"Why not? She's being mean to me on purpose now and getting away with it. I'm sick and tired of..."

"Stop! That's a dumb attitude, and I don't have time for dumb right now. I just bought two gallons of blue paint for the baby's room and haven't even finished laying on the primer coat yet. And there's the crib to put together, plus the lunar module stroller you ordered from that rip-off outfit online, and the car seat with its eight pages of instructions. You and Rose are going to have to make ugly faces at each other without involving me. I'm busy."

Anne put her hands on her hips and stuck out her baby bump. "In my circles, they call all that stuff you're doing nesting, only it's usually the mom."

"Look, when we decided it would be all cool and modern for me to be a stay-at-home dad, I drifted around in joy land for a week. That was before it dawned on me how much work it was going to be. Now I'm in panic mode. And the baby's room ain't gonna paint itself. What if he's born early?!"

"Okay, why don't I go annoy Pastor Seabrook with my problems, while you stay at home and paint walls and assemble things?"

"Good idea...if you don't expect too much from him. He's not the best counselor in the world, as you already know. Have you seen my drill? I have to anchor the baby's chest of drawers to the wall. We can't have it tipping over on him. And where's my set of screwdrivers?"

"Haven't seen them and wouldn't recognize them if I did." She paused and tried to think, a brain function that seemed to be growing weaker at the same rate her belly was growing rounder. "Not to beat the point," she said, "but I can't believe Rose is still freezing me out, and after I humbled myself before her like a worm."

"You don't sound humble to me," Gabe said. "You sound like a broken record."

"See there! I knew you and Rose were in cahoots. Now I have no choice but to go see Pastor Seabrook. He'll tell me what to do."

"No, he won't. He'll break a sweat praying for you, and then he'll make you work through your problem on your own. That's what preachers do. Have you seen my case of drill bits?"

❦

"Here I am again," Anne said as she settled her rotund torso into one of Pastor Seabrook's visitor chairs.

"Growing and glowing," he responded. "I've never seen you more beautiful. Better watch out, though. Don't forget what happened to Hannah after Samuel was born."

"Yeah, three more sons and two daughters. Six altogether, counting Samuel, a whole tent full of babies, one more than Rose has."

"Which brings to mind...how did your apology to Rose go? I remember she was high on your list."

"It didn't. She's still letting it hang in the air over my head like a dark cloud of rejection. It's beginning to stink."

"I told you that might happen, not the stink part, the rejection part. How are you handling it?"

"I did pretty well, at first. I was noble and patient. But then I started feeling hurt and put upon...you know, sorry for myself. But now I'm feeling mad, something I never felt once toward Rose over the years before I apologized. Guess I didn't care enough to get mad then in spite of her jabs. But today, here I am steaming."

"Maybe you resent giving her that little bit of power over you. The way things stand now, she can do whatever she chooses...forgive you, not forgive you, ignore you if she feels like it. It could go on indefinitely. Yep, you've given her control of the situation all right, and there's nothing you can do about it."

"There has to be something. Stop looking so smug and give me a hint. I know you've got a trick or two up your preacher's sleeve."

Pastor Seabrook laughed and nodded. "Is it that obvious? What you need to do now is put your anger aside and love Rose, genuinely and sincerely in thought, word, and deed."

"But she blocks me at every turn, acts like a cold fish."

"Which she is not. Her standoffishness is a self-protection mechanism. Which changes your responsibility not a whit. You need to go on loving her, regardless. Never quit. Never give up. That will put the ball in her court. She'll decide sooner or later if she wants to come around. But whether she does or doesn't, your job is to stay steady and pray for reconciliation, all the while trusting in God's good will. In other words, give the problem over to your Heavenly Father and leave it with him. Besides, you've got enough on your own plate without trying to run Rose's life. Didn't you say you were thinking about starting a support group for women struggling with infertility? Where are you with that?"

"Nowhere. I put it on hold until after the baby comes."

Pastor Seabrook looked thoughtful, contemplating for a moment the worthiness of Anne's excuse for not moving forward. He decided to challenge her thinking. "Hmm, I suppose I could see waiting until you get back on your feet before scheduling actual sessions, but why wait to start the planning phase? Listen, you came here wanting to know what to do about Rose. And now you know you have to keep loving her no matter what. Which brings you to a different question. What else should you be doing while Rose percolates? God might have something more in mind."

"Okay, okay, I get it. I'll stop obsessing about Rose and start reading up on how to run a prayer-based support group, although no one may ever show up. I'm thinking that not many infertile women want to know God's will for their lives. It's their will they're after. Don't get me wrong, though. I'm not sitting in judgment. How could I? I was one of them, and not very long ago."

⟨⟨⟨⟨

Nick and Sallie had been hosting the York family Sunday brunch for so long that none of the attendees could remember how the tradition got started. Lockstep is what Gabe called it. "You'd have to be taken hostage by space aliens to be excused from this drill," he had whispered to Anne on taking his seat for the first time at his mother-in-law's Sunday table.

"Hush and eat your fried green tomatoes," Anne had retorted. "Indigestion is a requirement, too."

The only hiccup that had ever thrown a sideways wrench into this hard and fast York family tradition was the marital meltdown between Thomas and Charlotte. Thomas' chair had gone suddenly empty after Little Annie was born with

Down's. But the ongoing discussions about the absence of the still beloved son-in-law were now taking a backseat to Anne and Gabe's baby announcement. And the closer the blessed event approached on the calendar, the more it dominated table talk. Every family member weighed in each week on the happy subject, except for Rose, who kept her mask of disinterest firmly in place as everyone else chattered with excitement.

"I'll be so glad when this baby finally gets here," Sallie said to Anne across the table on the Sunday marking one week until her due date. "I've been praying myself blue in the face ever since I found out about it. Seems like you've been pregnant two years."

"I agree," said Charlotte. "I've been praying nonstop, too. Have you finished painting the baby's room, Gabe? Must seem strange downsizing when you're adding a family member."

"Downsizing was the best thing we ever did," said Gabe. "Less space to vacuum, less to clean, less to paint. By the way, I've got half a gallon of baby-blue left over if anybody needs some matte latex."

"The baby's room isn't the only room Gabe has painted," Anne said. "He's been working like a dog refurbishing our fixer-upper, while I haven't been doing anything but taking care of my patients and preparing materials for when I start my new support group. We're both staying busy on purpose. It's how we keep from worrying ourselves sick about the baby. Paint, paint, paint. Work, work, work. Pray, pray, pray."

"Support group?" said Nick. "I thought you were done with those."

"Only the ones that don't allow prayer. It was pitiful how some of the women in that first group I participated in had to pray on the sly at home, behind the facilitator's back. The group I'm going to start - after the baby comes - will be one hundred percent prayer-based with a focus on seeking God's will."

Rose got an odd look after Anne's last comment. She made eye contact with her baby sister for the first time in months. "I didn't know you were planning to start a group like that," she said. "A friend in my *Bible* class - her name is Annette - has been trying to have a baby for years with no luck. She doesn't have a soul to talk to who has any professional understanding whatsoever of what she's going through, except for her doctor and the other personnel at his clinic. And they don't have time to do much listening."

"Not uncommon," Anne said. "I'd be honored if you'd let her know about the kind of group I'm planning to run. And she doesn't have to be a patient of mine to participate. Tell her that even if she's the only one who shows up when we kick off the group, I'll honor my commitment to schedule sessions. We'll have a group of two if it comes down to it."

Rose took her time responding. She looked into Anne's eyes as if no one else were at the table. "I'll give her the message," she said. "She needs a group, a praying group. And it'll make her feel less intimidated to know you and I are related. That alone will make all the difference."

— *Anne* —

God's timing is not my timing, for certain. Pastor Seabrook warned me that some people to whom I apologized for my inconsiderate behavior may not be willing to forgive me immediately, if ever. I thought I understood what he meant, until Rose rebuffed me for so long. But as it turned out, *long* in God's perspective was quite different from mine, particularly when it came to healing my relationship with Rose. It was yet another thing God had to teach me. Pastor Seabrook's words rang in my ears when Rose spoke to me at our mother's brunch table about her friend who was suffering from infertility. I knew without a doubt that God was showing me the beginning of a miracle. Rose was going to forgive me. All I had to do was love her no matter what, exactly as Pastor Seabrook had said. Moreover, our reconciliation did not have to take place all at once with tearful hugs and remorseful declarations. The second Rose made eye contact with me across our mother's brunch table, I knew we were on our way. I also knew we had no need to make an announcement. All we had to do was relax in the peace of the Holy Spirit and allow our miracle of reconciliation to flower over time. Rose made the process easy by redirecting our mutual attention toward the needs of someone else other than ourselves. God taught me in his perfect timing (not my own imperfect timing) that I had a great deal to learn from my sister. Thank you, God, for Rose. And thank you also for Pastor Seabrook, who taught me that all I had to do was love her, and you would do the rest.

Wait for the Lord; be strong,
and let your heart take courage; wait for the Lord!
PSALM 27:14 ESV

For still the vision awaits its appointed time;
it hastens to the end - it will not lie.
If it seems slow, wait for it: it will surely come;
it will not delay.
HABAKKUK 2:3 ESV

And let us not grow weary of doing good,
for in due season we will reap, if we do not give up.
GALATIANS 6:9 ESV

Chapter

31

Charlotte, Gabe, several nurses, and Anne's doctor encouraged her as she pushed through the final contraction of labor. When her baby emerged, everyone in the delivery room cheered as Anne's attending doctor made quick work of clipping and sealing the umbilical cord. "Congratulations," she said to the proud parents as the nurse placed the swaddled infant on Anne's chest. "You have a fine healthy baby girl."

Anne looked befuddled as she stared at her newborn's pink cap adorned with its huge pink knit bow. Gabe huddled near mother and child, laughing and crying. He encouraged his baby to hold onto his finger and kissed her sweet brow when she complied. "She's the most beautiful thing I've ever seen," Gabe said to Anne.

Anne's eyes were wide with shock. "But she's a girl. She was supposed to be a boy. Who would've thought it!?"

Gabe laughed so loud that the baby complained with a little mew. "Jesus would've thought it," said the jubilant new father.

Anne still could not grasp what had happened. "But the ultrasound," she said.

Gabe laughed aloud again at his good fortune. "Anne...

Annie, don't you see? King Jesus has just made it plain and clear that he's in charge of ultrasounds and everything else. He's given us a daughter with girl-power."

Anne smiled through joyful tears as she hugged her baby and her loving husband. "Thank you, Jesus." she whispered. "Thank you, thank you, thank you!"

Anne and Gabe - fresh out of labor and delivery and now secluded in Anne's hospital room - were still marveling over their first child when Charlotte's daughter, Little Annie, opened the door and held it back for her mother to push an empty wheelchair inside. Little Annie smiled and ran to Anne's bedside. She stroked the baby's pink blanket and then touched her own ear.

"Oh, yes, sweetheart," Charlotte said to Little Annie. "God hears our prayers all right. Your precious new cousin is proof of that. And she's a girl like you, a wonderful surprise."

Anne held her baby at a lower angle so that Little Annie could get a closer look. The newest tiny York girl yawned, which made Little Annie giggle and point. Even with Gabe's help, Anne had a bit of trouble doing two things at once... monitoring the visit between the two young cousins and carrying on a sane conversation with Charlotte. "What did you find out?" she asked her sister. "Will they let us go?"

Charlotte couldn't answer for a moment. She was too distracted by the difficulty of maneuvering the wheelchair closer to Anne's bed. Gabe took over her effort, freeing her to talk with Anne. "I didn't ask. Thought it would be better to plead forgiveness later than permission now."

Anne looked apprehensive. "Can we get by the nurse's station without a problem? Do you think?"

Charlotte leaned past Little Annie's shoulder and took a long, loving look at the newborn's pink face. "We'll be fine," she said to Anne without taking her eyes off the baby. "They'll assume that a doctor – *you!* – would have better sense than to leave the building with a newborn...against all rules."

Anne glanced at Gabe, who interpreted her look as his cue to take the baby. He held his swaddled child and stood to the side as Charlotte helped Anne into the wheelchair. Little Annie continued petting the baby's pink blanket. Gabe handed the small bundle back to Anne in the wheelchair. "All we have to do is act normal," he said to the anxious group. "As long as the baby is with her mama, no one will suspect a thing."

⚜

Gabe pushed the wheelchair bearing Anne and her baby girl out of the room into the main hallway of the maternity wing. Charlotte and Little Annie followed as he headed toward the nurses' station. Charlotte heeded Gabe's admonition to act normal...almost. The nurse in charge of the station smiled as they filed by. "Hey, y'all," she said. "Taking the little one on a stroll? Appreciate it if you stay on the floor, please. Rules."

Anne responded casually. "Yeah, rules. We had to get out of that stuffy room a few minutes, breathe some different air."

The nurse agreed with a dramatic nod. "Oh, I get that totally," she said, fanning away a hot flash with a manila folder. She smiled as her gaze alighted again on the baby in Anne's arms. "Would you look at that little chicky? Six hours old and already going on a joyride. A York girl for ya, huh. Y'all stay on the floor now, you hear?"

Anne held her baby closer, nodding and smiling with faux goodwill. Little Annie chuckled and waved to the nurse, who waved back with a big grin. Gabe and Charlotte stared straight ahead as they marched down the hall like robots. Both had guilty looks. Little Annie and the baby were the only ones succeeding at acting normal.

Anne continued her fake-chatty exchange with the nurse. "See you in a bit," she called as Gabe pushed the wheelchair faster. "Just going to breathe some different air."

As the chair reached the bank of elevators at the far end of the hallway, a second nurse arrived at the central workstation and engaged the first in conversation. Gabe used the distraction to push the DOWN button on the middle elevator and scoot the wheelchair inside. Charlotte and Little Annie crowded in behind. The door closed everyone in with a whoosh, with neither nurse realizing a thing.

When the elevator reached the lobby, its door opened again, revealing Charlotte and Little Annie now facing forward, the wheelchair bearing Anne and the baby wedged in behind them, and Gabe squashed flat against the back wall.

Charlotte peeked out at the reception desk manned by three elderly volunteers, one of whom spied her. Charlotte signaled Gabe and Anne to wait. She took Little Annie's hand and tugged her toward the desk, where she diverted the volunteers' attention with her daughter's cuteness.

Gabe then sneaked a look and seized the opportunity. He

wheeled the chair out of the elevator and walked at a fast clip toward the automatic double doors of the front entrance. On exiting, he began a slow jog, steering the wheelchair carefully along the sidewalk. Anne leaned forward in the chair, clutching her baby girl to her chest, looking determined in a peculiar manner. Passersby yielded to the wheelchair, although several appeared concerned on seeing Anne in a hospital gown, holding a swaddled newborn, looking like a run-away maternity patient.

Charlotte and Little Annie soon burst through the same automatic doors that Gabe, Anne, and the baby had just escaped. Charlotte grabbed Little Annie's hand and dragged her in a trot toward the jogging Gabe, who was now moving too fast for them to overtake. Little Annie looked ready to cry. It was then that Thomas, her father, appeared out of nowhere at her mother's side. He gave Charlotte a meaningful look and swung Little Annie up to his hip. With Thomas carrying Little Annie, the three lagging followers were able to catch up with Gabe and the speeding wheelchair.

All five fugitives, plus Thomas, the added sixth, moved swiftly across the next street via the pedestrian lane to the sidewalk on the other side, along which they hurried until they reached the next busy intersection, where a police officer held traffic long enough for them to cross.

A short block later, the odd entourage arrived at the building of their destination, Savannah's Cancer Treatment and Research Center. A stranger held the door open for the perspiring Gabe to roll the wheelchair inside. Charlotte, Thomas, and Little Annie followed, with Thomas still carrying Little Annie. He did not let her down to walk on her own until they had made their way by elevator to the correct floor. Whereupon Gabe soon found Nick's room number, and they entered one by one...Anne and the baby first, pushed in the wheelchair by Gabe, and then Charlotte, Little Annie, and Thomas last.

Anne gasped when she saw how ashen her father looked as he lay sleeping in his hospital bed. Sallie and Rose huddled close by, watching over him like two guardian angels. Sallie looked old and weary. Rose did not look much better. She appeared to have been weeping, puffy-eyed and red-faced. William, Rose's husband, stood by the window apart from his wife, mother-in-law, and sleeping father-in-law.

"Hey," Anne said softly to her mother.

Sallie stretched her eyes wide at the sight of Anne and the baby in the wheelchair. "Anne, honey," she said. "How did you ever...? Your baby...not a day old yet."

Anne responded in a whisper. "I had to see Daddy. Has he been awake today?"

"In and out," Sallie said, still shocked and surprised by Anne's presence. "Mostly out, though. Oh, my goodness, Charlotte and Little Annie...and Thomas, too."

Thomas nodded, making it a point to take Charlotte's hand in his and smile at Sallie, who smiled back with understanding.

Anne stared at the sleeping Nick. Gabe kept his hands on the back handles of the wheelchair, waiting for further instructions from his wife. "Roll me a little closer, Gabe?" she said. "Maybe he'll come around."

Gabe pushed the wheelchair to Nick's bedside. Anne spoke to her father. "Can you hear me, Daddy? I brought somebody to meet you."

Nick stirred and opened his eyes. He smiled and reached out to touch Anne's cheek. "Hey there, slugger," he said to his youngest daughter. "How're you doing today?"

"I'm fine, Daddy. Look who's with me." Weeping openly now, she held up her newborn in Nick's line of vision, then she laid the baby on the hospital bed just below her father's pillow. "She was born a couple of hours ago. Isn't she beautiful? We already named her Sallie, after Mom."

Anne glanced in her mother's direction. Sallie smiled at her through tears that flowed now out of joy and gratitude instead of pain. Unaware of this small communication between Anne and her mother, Nick said sweetly, "You could have searched the world over and not found a more beautiful name. She looks like every one of you York girls when you were first born, pretty as a picture."

Tears rolled down Anne's cheeks too fast for her to wipe them away. "I couldn't wait for you to see her, Dad. I knew you would be glad, even if she isn't a grandson. We thought for sure she was going to be a boy. Everyone did. My doctor, everyone. But she's not! She's our little girl!"

"Goes to show you, slugger. God has a sense of humor. I'm overjoyed for you, Annie, same as I was for Rose and Charlotte when their babies were born. Seven granddaughters! I am a blessed man. Now I know why the number seven represents perfection in the Good Book. Hey, is that Little Annie over there? Give Grandpa a hug, sweetheart. And Thomas came, too? Long time no see, Tom. Welcome back. Hope you're home to stay."

Thomas smiled and nodded. He put an arm around

Charlotte and pulled her closer. Little Annie ran to Nick's bedside. Anne rolled the wheelchair a few inches away from the bed to make room for Little Annie to hug Nick. Nick patted the child's small back as she kissed him. Little Annie let go of Nick and stroked baby Sallie's pink blanket. She turned and smiled at Anne, then scampered back over to stand with Charlotte and Thomas.

Nick struggled to speak again through a rattling cough. "'*Proverbs 17:6. Grandchildren are the crown of old men.*'"

Sallie put a hand on her sick husband's shoulder. "Stop talking, Nick, honey. It saps your strength."

Anne tried to ease her father's exhaustion. "How about we pray together, Dad...and not chat. I'll hold the baby close to you, so she'll learn you're her grandpa. She's a consecrated baby, you know. Gabe and I promised God."

Sallie made eye contact with the weeping Charlotte. "Stop crying, dear. We need you to pray, especially for Anne. She's in no better shape than your father."

Anne did not give Charlotte a chance to answer Sallie. "No, Mom," she said. "I want to pray this time." She clamped her eyes shut, keeping one hand on the baby for safety. "*Dear God, thank you for giving Gabe and me a daughter. And thank you for the love of Daddy and Mama and Charlotte and Rose and their husbands, William and Thomas, and all their children. I know I'm the lowest of low on that list, Lord, way under everyone else, and I thank you for that, too...and for finding a way to use me no matter how low I am. We know our new baby belongs to you, Jesus. Please help Gabe and me bring her up right. In your holy name, I pray. Amen.*"

Sallie and Charlotte could not control their tears while

Anne prayed, but when the monitor attached to Nick stopped beeping and began an ominous buzzing sound, everyone in the room froze with fear.

A nurse rushed in and began working on Nick. She paused only long enough to scoop up the baby and hand her to Anne. Two other nurses arrived to help, though it was too late. After a few moments, all three stepped back from Nick's bed and allowed Sallie to collapse sobbing over her dead husband.

Anne, now oddly calm and collected, watched her mother cry over her father. Staying back out of respect for her mother's grief, she tucked baby Sallie close to her chest with one hand and held out the other to Gabe, who stepped nearer the wheelchair and put his arm around his wife's shoulders. Anne gripped Gabe's hand for security and strength.

Charlotte and Thomas leaned down and comforted Little Annie, who kept touching her ear, her sign for God hears. And William moved closer to Rose so that she could lean on his chest and weep.

— *Anne* —

God called my dad home in the perfect fullness of his own timing. I was able to understand and accept this Truth even through my grief as I and everyone else in the cold, clinical atmosphere of the hospital room observed the peaceful departure of Nick York...beloved husband, father, grandfather, and father-in-law. His passing occurred right on time, same as everything else on God's schedule. Perfect timing is one of our Lord's Spiritual mysteries, the details of which we humans cannot fathom. Yet we rest in him in faith, a capacity that is also a gift, as we trust peacefully all is well in his Kingdom. The closer I grow to God, the more I marvel at the mystery of how he entwines his flawless will and timing through the individual and collective lives of those who love him. We are part of his colorful family tapestry, his holy warp and weft as he weaves us together, beginning and ending with the holiest thread of all, his one and only Son, Jesus. Thus, as my dad left us that day, and as he and those at his bedside experienced his departure in our individual ways, I thanked God for being in charge of the best for each one of us, plus our best as a group. *Thank you, Jesus, for easing our pain with the peace that comes from trusting in God Almighty. Oh, Lord Jesus, we also thank you that your peace is most restful and healing when we live our lives in harmony with you. Amen.*

And we know that God causes everything to work together
for the good of those who love God and are called
according to his purpose for them. For God knew his people
in advance, and he chose them to become like his son,
so that his son would be the firstborn among many
brothers and sisters. And having chosen them, he called
them to come to him. And having given them right

standing, he gave them his glory.
ROMANS 8:28-30 NLT

Chapter

32

Anne, wearing a white lab coat and reading glasses complete with tacky neck chain, sat at her office desk going over paperwork in a folder. Someone rapped at her door. "Come in," she called without taking her eyes off her work.

The door creaked open. Timidly, Rose peeped around it. "Hi...do you have a minute?" she said.

Anne looked up, puzzled by the presence of her eldest sister, who had never visited her office before. "Uhh...sure, Rose. Come in. What's up? Nothing wrong, I hope."

"No, no. Everything is good." Rose walked over and placed a small stack of greeting card envelopes on Anne's desk before taking a seat. "Your receptionist - Carmen, right? - asked me to bring you today's mail. Looks like more sympathy cards. I've got a stack of my own at home."

Anne leaned forward and picked up the top card. She examined the return address, her eyes melancholy. "People of Savannah have been so kind about Daddy. It's like they wanted to send messages to him, but couldn't, so they had to send them to us...second best."

Rose hesitated, choosing her words. After a long pause, she said, "I came over to offer to help you with your new support group, if you can use me."

Anne placed the envelope back on the stack, took off her glasses, and gave Rose her full attention. "You have no idea how much I appreciate that. Truly, I do, but who knows if anyone even saw the announcement on my pitiful little sign out front?"

Rose looked down at her hands before resuming eye contact with Anne. "I didn't really come over here to talk about the group or your sign, although I would like to try to help if I can. My friend, Annette, called me last night and said she plans to attend today. That gives you one guaranteed participant." Rose took another break, accompanied by a labored sigh. Then she summoned her courage and went on. "My real reason for coming was to tell you something I've already told Mom and Charlotte."

"Let me guess," Anne said. "You're pregnant! With triplets, quadruplets, quintuplets!"

"Don't wish it on me. With my history, it could happen. No, I came to say I don't hold anything against Daddy anymore, or you, or anyone else, including myself. All I want from here on out is to take care of Mom and be a decent role model for my daughters and nieces, and for you and Charlotte, too. It's my responsibility as the oldest. I just wish I'd told Daddy before he died."

"You didn't have to, Rose. He already knew, because he knew you." Anne grinned with a loving twinkle in her eye. "You were his favorite, after all."

Rose laughed. She looked relieved to have shared her new life intentions for the future. "Somehow, we were all his favorites, weren't we?" she said. "Separately and together."

Anne glanced at her wall clock. "Time to launch my nonexistent support group," she said. "Let's go see if anyone showed up besides Annette."

❦

Anne and Rose stood in her office waiting room, looking with surprised faces at the line of women stretching from the reception window to the entrance of the building and out the door. "Dr. York, this is impossible," said Carmen. "We don't have enough room for all these people."

Rose gave the first woman in line a hug. "Annette, hi," she said. "This is my sister, Anne, leader of the group, or groups, considering the size of this crowd."

Anne was in too much shock to offer a proper hello to Rose's friend. As she gaped at the sheer number of beautiful women in the line, she spied Renee and Maureen near the front entryway. Renee waved to her, smiling. Maureen stood behind Renee, her expression serious in stark contrast to that of her enthusiastic companion.

"Hi...hello," Renee shouted to Anne. "Looks like you've got a lot of takers today. Remember us? Maureen and me. I'm Renee...from Lucinda's group?"

Anne, followed by Rose, walked in quickstep toward the two women. "I'm so glad to see you both," Anne said to her old acquaintances, genuinely pleased they had come. "But Maureen, are you sure this type of group is for you, prayer-based?"

"I've changed my mind about prayer...about a lot of things," said Maureen, her attitude no longer argumentative.

"What I need now is forgiveness. Renee convinced me."

Anne took Maureen's hands in hers in a manner reminiscent of Sallie. "You and me both, girlfriend. And Renee, too. We'll ask God's forgiveness as a trio."

"Yep," said Renee, "the three of us along with that mob on your front walk. Have you seen what's going on out there?"

Anne and Rose looked at each other with a trace of alarm, then exited the front door in solidarity. No longer did Anne have to wonder if anyone had seen her homemade sign:

DR. ANNE YORK, OB/GYN, NOW OFFERING CHRISTIAN SUPPORT GROUPS FOR WOMEN SUFFERING FROM INFERTILITY. FOCUS WILL BE ON DISCERNING GOD'S WILL FOR YOUR FAMILY THROUGH PRAYER.

A huge crowd of women stood outside the office, talking quietly together as they waited. They had spaced themselves in little knots of twos and threes down the walkway, on the sidewalk, on the lawn, and down the street. Sallie stood on the grass near the corner of the building, minding Anne's baby in a stroller and also Little Sallie, who was entertaining herself with a coloring book and crayons at her grandmother's feet.

Anne spied Charlotte moving from group to group in the crowd, attempting to reassure everyone that instructions on what to do next were forthcoming. Gabe, wearing a black t-shirt with white lettering on the front and back reading *STAY-AT-HOME DAD*, was busy helping Thomas set up two card tables to create a makeshift reception area.

Anne rushed over to Charlotte. "What in the world?" she said. "How did this happen?!"

Charlotte got a guilty look. "I...uh...sort of ran an ad in the *Savannah Morning News* with the same message as your sign there...sort of."

Anne stretched her eyes wide. "You did what...*sort of?!*" To be heard, Anne was forced to speak louder than she would have liked. The crowd noise was increasing. Anne's sheer volume frightened Charlotte, whose own voice turned squeaky as she tried to explain herself. "I've been running it for a week, trying to get the word out. Did a pretty good job, huh. Look at all these takers, way more than that pitiful sign of yours would have ever attracted."

"Okay, okay, I get it, thanks," Anne said, grateful, flustered, overwrought. "But now we have to roll with the chaos."

Gabe appeared at her side, an angel to her rescue. "Gabe!" she said. "Could you bring a chair out of the office for me to stand on? I have to speak to these women. Rose, please...go back inside and get some pens and a stack of index cards from Carmen...two stacks! And tell her to take down the women's contact information as they come through the line inside and promise them call-backs. You and Charlotte can catch the ones out here."

Gabe placed a chair from Anne's waiting room in front of her. She stepped up on it with shaky balance and began shouting over the crowd. "Everyone! Everyone! Can you hear me? I'm Dr. Anne York, OB/GYN, and this is my office. Looks like we're in agreement about what kind of help we need to cope with infertility issues...support groups based on prayer and God's involvement. Am I reading you right? Are you here looking for God's will in your lives?"

One woman called out of the crowd in a loud voice. "Absolutely! We know God hears us! Now we want to hear Him!"

More women shouted agreement. "Yes! Right! We want to hear God through the Word and prayer, *yes!*"

Anne smiled down at the women's hopeful faces. "Good, good," she said. "Then let's work together forming lines: one for inside the building, and two for the card tables out here. We'll take down your phone numbers and email addresses and get back in touch to schedule you into small groups. My sisters will be manning the outdoor tables. Does anyone want to have prayer before we start?"

"We do! We do!" several women yelled out popcorn style. "Prayer! Yes!"

"Okay, quiet then," Anne said, and she waited while the sweet hush of the Holy Spirit enveloped the lovely crowd. The women bowed their heads in unity as Anne prayed. "Dear Jesus, Holy Spirit, Father God, please comfort the aching hearts of your servants here today with grace and mercy. Help each one find your will for her life and family. We trust you, Lord, and we're here to listen to you in obedience. As our sister in Christ said earlier, we know that you hear us, God. Now please, please help us hear you. Give us wisdom as we seek discernment. In the name of Jesus, we pray with the Holy Spirit. Amen."

In unison, the crowd cheered and wept as they cried out in their melodic feminine voices, "Amen, amen, amen!"

Anne stepped down from the box and began helping Gabe and Thomas with organizing the three lines. Rose and Charlotte took their seats at the card tables and began writing down information woman by woman. Anne smiled as she worked the eager crowd, chatting warmly with individuals, encouraging all, extending her hand, giving hugs. Everyone was relieved when two med techs from the office brought out coolers filled with water bottles and began distributing them.

It was then Pastor Seabrook drove up in his vintage Cadillac and parked at the curb. He emerged from his Caddy a happy man, smiling and looking smart in his black jacket and white minister's collar. He moved immediately to the center of the action and began focusing on individuals in the long lines. At first, Anne did not realize he had arrived, but when she spotted him talking compassionately and earnestly with various women in the crowd, she halted her own conversations and watched him. His heartfelt manner tugged at her heart. She walked over and patted his stooped shoulder. "You were right," she said to her dear old counselor. "God wanted me to stop focusing on myself and turn around to see everybody else's needs." She laughed when someone in the crowd accidentally jostled her against the old man, causing them to have to hold onto one another to keep from falling.

Pastor Seabrook's hearty laugh echoed pure joy as he said to his favorite counselee, "But who knew you'd be facing a multitude?"

"Not by myself, though," Anne responded. "Jesus himself, along with you and my family...you're all here to face it with me."

"You're counting me as a part of your crazy clan?"

"You bet your life I am. Now get over to those card tables and start working your way down Rose's line. May as well get acquainted with everyone. You know you're going to have to act as facilitator in a few groups. I'll keep moving down Charlotte's line. Every woman here needs a personal welcome. Let's make sure they get one."

Pastor Seabrook grinned. "Guess we were right about the ministry God had mind for you, besides being a wife and mother."

Anne took Pastor Seabrook by his arm and turned him around one-hundred-and-eighty degrees. She gave him a gentle nudge toward Rose's table. "Enough about me," she said. "Go find out what God has in mind for you!"

— *Anne* —

Imagine that, a newly reformed sinner like me giving march-ing orders to a seasoned believer like Pastor Seabrook. *"Go find out what God has in mind for you!"* And more surprising, the seasoned believer submitting to my bossiness by walking straight to Rose's table to find out what God did, indeed, *have in mind for him,* living proof of our Heavenly Father's determination to glorify himself by using the faithful and the weak to further his kingdom. Believe me, if God, who can choose anyone he pleases, decides to use someone as inept as me as a spiritual encourager, he can use anybody. That is one of the nice things I learned after he healed my Spiritual tone deafness. The moment I began praying, reading my *Bible,* and seeking out the company of fellow believers, I found myself able to hear the Father's voice more clearly. And from there flowed everything else. Paul, the apostle, would say the Holy Spirit gave me the mind of Christ when I confessed my sins, begged forgiveness, and repented (admitting that I have to go back to God's throne every day to ask forgiveness for new sins driven by self). Paul had many comforting words to say to new believers back in the day about the mind of Christ. He was talking to you and me, as well. Listen with your Spiritual ears to his explanation in *1 Corinthians* so that you can hear him speaking directly to you. If you listen to Paul and heed God's teachings, you can have the mind of Christ and understand his instructions. That is God's promise to you. CLAIM IT!

[Paul] *For, "Who can know the Lord's thoughts? Who knows enough to teach him?" But we understand these things, for we have the mind of Christ.*

1 Corinthians 2:16 NLT

Father God, this is Anne again, asking you to remind us to listen for your voice as you speak out your expectations for our humble obedience. Your Holy Spirit always *hears us* calling to you, Lord Jesus. We thank you now for empowering your loving servants to *hear you!* In your name, God's Son and my Savior, amen.

HAPPIEST OF ENDINGS

Women's Ministry Directors, Sunday School Teachers, Bible Study Leaders, Retreat and Conference Planners —

Terry Ward Tucker has made your job of finding fresh training materials and a new speaker much easier by creating a discovery guide to accompany MOON RIVER. Tucker designed the guide to help groups (and individuals) enhance their prayer times, hence the title:

GOD HEARS YOU! DO YOU HEAR GOD?
Transform Your Prayer Life from Self-Centered to God-Centered.

Whether you choose to enjoy the novel and study guide as stand-alones or a set of two, your prayer life will be blessed by getting to know MOON RIVER's quirky characters and using the guide to examine prayer solutions to their problems and your own! Interactive, Scripture-based activities and readings ensure rewarding growth in two fundamental Truths:

1. Prayer is a massively valuable God-gift in the life of every Christian who wants a warmer connection with the Father, Son, and Holy Spirit.

2. And the surest way to enhance that connection is to SEEK GOD consistently in prayer, Scripture, and the company of other believers.

JOIN OUR STUDY AND GROW CLOSER TO GOD. YOUR GROUPS WILL LOVE IT!

Contact Information:
TerryWardTucker@gmail.com 803-320-1247

More Works by Tucker
(partial list)

INSPIRE YOU Daily Devotions

Moonbow Over Charleston

Charleston Kisses

Moonlight & Mill Whistles

Charleston's Elegant Sinners
2023 pub date

Arlena Returns to Charleston
2023 pub date

Only God Can
feature film - screenplay co-writer

Radiance of Jesus: One Hundred Devotions

Fragrance of Jesus: One Hundred Devotions
2022 pub date

Magnificence of Jesus
2023 pub date

Terry Ward Tucker and her family are members of First Baptist Church in Charleston, SC. She holds a PhD in Reading Education. MOON RIVER, her newest novel, is set in Savannah, Georgia. MOON RIVER is unique in that Tucker composed an optional discovery guide on prayer - GOD HEARS YOU! DO YOU HEAR GOD? - to accompany the book. Individuals and groups can enjoy the novel and guide as stand-alones or a set of two.

Tucker's popular devotional, INSPIRE YOU *Daily Devotions*, was so well received by readers that she responded to their encouragement by writing RADIANCE OF JESUS: *One Hundred Devotions*, the first title in a series for those who enjoy worshiping on the same page together, plus anyone else who wants to be blessed mightily by God's *SonLight*. Her second book in the series, FRAGRANCE OF JESUS: *One Hundred Devotions*, will launch in 2022, and the third, MAGNIFICENCE OF JESUS, in 2023.

Tucker's first novel, *Charleston's Elegant Sinners*, is set in the Lowcountry of South Carolina. Her second, *Moonlight and Mill Whistles*, received *ForeWord Magazine*'s Silver Book of the Year Award. Winston Groom, author of *Forrest Gump*, wrote, "Terry Ward Tucker tells a lovely and captivating story in *Moonlight and Mill Whistles*. Her writing is a joy to read." Tucker's novel, *Moonbow Over Charleston*, is also set in the South. Pat Conroy wrote about *Moonbow*, "Terry Ward Tucker paints a moonbow upon Charleston's night sky and gifts us all with its loveliness. Thank you, Terry!"

Tucker served as screenplay co-writer for faith-based movie, *Only God Can*, produced by Inspire You Entertainment, and screenplay writer for *Hate Won't Win*, a new film in development based on the shooting massacre at Mother Emanuel Church in Charleston. Terry came to Christ at age eight in a revival meeting at First Baptist Church in Lancaster, SC. She is thankful to be known as a born again Christian and hopes people all over the world will be as blessed by reading her daily devotions as she was by writing them.

Made in the USA
Columbia, SC
18 February 2023

12492384R10169